Excerpt:

His sweet sexy smile
mesmerized by his full lips. S
word he spoke. A sudden uncomfortable rush came over her.
Dinner was one thing; there they were in a public place, but
now they were alone outside her hotel suite door. The hunger
in his eyes ran deep through her soul. His scent invigorated
her senses. Part of her wanted to run, to hide, and part of her
ached to be at his side.

She desperately fought the urge to delve into the kiss
she sensed he wanted. A kiss she desired. He stirred hidden
desires in her like an erupting volcano. His fingers touched
her bare shoulder. She shivered with his touch. The tips of
his fingers traced her arm and stopped at her hip. One simple
touch sent sensual vibrations throughout her body. His
tongue touched his lip. The gesture weakened her thought to
go inside. His lips merely inches away from hers, Meghan's
lips parted to invite his kiss. He moved in closer to her.

"May I?" he asked and his finger slightly touched
her lip. She nodded. His lips met hers. His tongue lightly
followed the outline of her bottom lip. Meghan moved closer
to him inviting the kiss to deepen and he followed her lead.
Her hand touched his chest, her fingers strong against him;
she could feel his heartbeat. The sun's rays beamed through
the windows of her suite window. Her first thought was, *that
was an unforgettable kiss.* No one ever kissed Meghan that
passionately before. For the first time she felt alive, desired
and desperately wanted.

Angela Ford

Unforgettable Kiss

Angela Ford

Angela Ford

Angela Ford

Books to Go Now Publication

ISBN-13:978-1495479571

ISBN-10:1495479579

Look for Other Stories by Angela Ford
Closure

DEDICATION

Dedicated to my amazing parents for their love that
keeps me believing, fairy tales do exist.
And to my amazing children, Devon &
Shaylyn…mummy loves you xoxo

Chapter One

The beauty of the golf course that overlooked the Santa Catalina Mountains made it hard for Meghan to resist. It had been some time since she'd enjoyed a game—or anything, for that matter. The resort's Club Attendant promised to match her with a partner. She waited at the first tee.

"Excuse me, are you Ms. Eden?" Meghan turned.

"Yes, I'm Meghan Eden," she said and extended her hand. There was a long pause. She waited for an introduction from the man who stood before her. She smiled. He had not let go of her hand. He did not speak. She raised an eyebrow and tilted her head to break the silence.

"I am sorry. Please forgive me. Your eyes took me off-guard. I've never seen such a brilliant blue. They sparkle like sapphires." He let go of her hand.

"Thank you," she politely replied. "And you are Mr. Nolan?" she asked.

"Again, I'm sorry. Please excuse my manners. I'm Eric Nolan," he said.

"It's a gorgeous day for a game. It's been awhile since I played so I may be a little rusty," Meghan honestly informed him. She wasn't sure how to take this man. He was definitely candy to the eye but he appeared to be lacking the self-confidence that usually went hand-in-hand with a great looking guy. *Maybe he's just shy or perhaps this is his way of a pick-up.* Meghan chuckled to herself and wondered if it really mattered. She had only dated one man, her ex-husband. She swore after him she would never attempt love again.

"I can't remember the last time I played, so it looks like the club's attendant made the right choice when he paired us." Eric grabbed his driver from his golf bag.

"You are going to tee-off with a driver?" Meghan questioned him.

"To gain distance," he replied as he set the tee into the ground and placed the golf ball in position. She watched him bend over and caught herself. He stood only inches from her. The scent of his cologne played with her senses. Meghan lost her train of thought. She wondered if he had noticed she drifted for a moment. He spoke respectfully even if he had noticed, "Ladies first". Meghan chose the wood from her bag, "I may not get the distance but I'll get it straight". She smiled with confidence. For some strange reason she felt at ease with a man she just met.

After the second hole she felt like they had connected personally and competitively. Eric hadn't even shocked her when he bet on their game with the cost of dinner. She felt she had a new friend and by the time they hit the third hole she mentioned he could call her Meg as her friends did.

"Meg, I've never had this much fun since, well, I can't remember." He laughed.

"Same. It's been a long time," she admitted.

"You make me feel like an ordinary guy," he confessed.

"Thank you, I think," she said and laughed.

"What I mean is," he continued, "I know we've agreed to dinner tonight but I want to be honest with you—"

Here it comes, the letdown. She interrupted him. "It's okay if you don't want to."

"No, I want to. I just want to be completely honest with you about who I am. I'm just surprised that you don't know. I take it you never go to the movies?" he asked.

She shook her head. Now she was curious. He named a few movies and she shook her head again. "I'm sorry," she said.

"Don't be sorry. I'm glad you like me for who I am, not what I've become," he told her. "I have always wanted to be an actor. A few years back I got a break and then it happened so fast. It was like overnight success and since then my life has become so chaotic that I haven't had the chance to breathe. Last night I walked off the set. I had to get away from the crazy world I live in."

She smiled. She *did* like him. He seemed like a decent man. She'd had a lot of fun with him on the golf course. He touched her heart with the emotions he had shared. She could only imagine what that lifestyle would do to a person.

"Can we still have dinner?" he asked.

"I never back out of a promise," Meghan agreed but wondered what she was getting into. She was a private person.

Meghan won and kept her promise. One game of golf, one dinner, but Meghan felt comfortable with him. It felt like they were old friends catching up, despite the interruptions for Eric's autograph. She liked his caring nature he gave to his fans. They had an amazing connection. After dinner Eric asked to walk her back to her suite. She clutched her purse and searched for her key, "I should go inside." Eric reached for her hand and stopped her search. "Not yet," he whispered against that soft spot behind her ear. He stood back and smiled. His sweet sexy smile melted her. Meghan was mesmerized by his full lips. She watched them form each word he spoke. A sudden uncomfortable rush came over her. Dinner was one thing; there they were in a public place, but now they were alone outside her hotel suite door. The hunger in his eyes ran deep through her soul. His scent invigorated her senses. Part of her wanted to run, to hide, and part of her ached to be at his side.

She desperately fought the urge to delve into the kiss she sensed he wanted. A kiss she desired. He stirred hidden desires in her like an erupting volcano. His fingers touched her bare shoulder. She shivered with his touch. The tips of his fingers traced her arm and stopped at her hip. One simple touch sent sensual vibrations throughout her body. His tongue touched his lip. The gesture weakened her thought to go inside. His lips merely inches away from hers, Meghan's lips parted to invite his kiss. He moved in closer to her.

"May I?" he asked and his finger slightly touched her lip. She nodded. His lips met hers. His tongue lightly followed the outline of her bottom lip. Meghan moved closer to him inviting the kiss to deepen and he followed her lead. Her hand touched his chest, her fingers strong against him; she could feel his heartbeat.

The sun's rays beamed through the windows of her suite window. Her first thought was, *that was an unforgettable kiss.* No one ever kissed Meghan that passionately before. For the first time she felt alive, desired and desperately wanted. She looked at the clock at her bedside: *7:05.* She jumped out of bed and was showered with coffee in hand by seven-thirty. The terrace of her suite overlooked the beauty of the golf course. Eric and she had agreed on a re-match for eight o'clock. He hadn't come by or called. Reality hit her that he wasn't coming. *Why would he?* She wondered. Meghan turned when she heard a knock at the door.

"Oh," she said sadly.

"Oh? That's all I get," Paige asked and walked past Meghan. "No, 'Good Morning Paige'?" she asked sarcastically. Paige poured a coffee and turned to her friend. "So?"

"Sorry Paige, good morning," Meghan replied.

"That's not what I meant, Meg," Paige said with a laugh. "How was dinner with the movie star?"

"Dinner with Eric was good. His kiss good night was unforgettable," Meghan sighed.

"And?"

"And nothing." He asked for a re-match of golf for—" Meghan paused and looked at her watch for the second time in the last five minutes—"eight o'clock this morning".

"Unforgettable." Paige grinned then asked, "What the hell are you doing here then?"

"He said he'd meet me here." Meghan walked out to the terrace and Paige followed. Paige put her arm around Meghan. "Maybe he slept in."

"I don't think he's coming. Why would he? Who am I to him?" Meghan rambled. She was a small-town woman with a small-town business, 'Body & Soul Spa' which she co-owned with Paige. Eric Nolan was the most famous eligible bachelor. Meghan had no idea who Eric Nolan was when the resort's attendant gave her his name. She never watched television or went to the movies. She read if she had time. She was too busy wrapped up in her own business. Paige informed her he was the most sought after actor in Hollywood. Over dinner, Eric talked about his last few films and by what Paige told her, they had made him an icon in the movie industry and the most eligible bachelor in the hearts of many women across the globe.

"You were the one who didn't care who he was. You were the one who didn't even want to go to dinner with Eric Nolan," Paige stressed his name. She knew who he was. Famous people always fascinated Paige.

"I said I didn't know who he was when I first met him," Meghan corrected her. Paige had refused to golf with her and went for a massage when their seminar ended.

"You're a little testy this morning. That was some kiss," Paige teased her.

"And I didn't want to go to dinner at first. You pushed me out the door," Meghan reminded her.

"Because you never have fun Meg, and he's a movie star," Paige stressed again.

Meghan just rolled her eyes, "Why would he want to see me again Paige? Seriously, I'm no one to him. There are probably hundreds of women he'd rather be with." Meghan grabbed her purse. "Let's go for breakfast. I'm hungry," Meghan held the door open and waited for Paige.

"You always eat when you're stressed," Paige announced as she walked past. Meghan had mumbled something but Paige kept walking toward the elevator.

Paige finally heard the details of dinner and the kiss over breakfast.

"I wish I hadn't gone to dinner with him Paige." Meghan continuously straightened her napkin on her lap. Paige rolled her eyes, "The look on your face when you first opened the door this morning tells me different". She knew Paige was right but that only made her thoughts drift.

That damn kiss was etched in her mind. She swore to Paige she would never attempt that again. Meghan couldn't get it out of her mind but it was torture to her heart. She hadn't allowed her heart to feel anything in so long. She had been safe. Now she was a wreck. Meghan hadn't been with a man since her husband destroyed her life. She would never forget the words that came from the police officer that night. *There's been a terrible accident. Your son has been killed and your husband is in critical condition at Mercy General.* Since that night Meghan vowed she would never trust or love again.

Their flight was at four o'clock that afternoon. Meghan was quiet for the most of the day except for their discussion about the Spa and what they had gathered from the seminar the day before. Her mind kept drifting back to that kiss and Eric. She told herself that he was famous and had probably kissed many women. Meghan wondered if the kiss meant anything to him. She tried to erase the thought of him and the kiss from her mind and focus on the business, as she had for the past few years. The pain in her heart from her loss was real. Work helped.

Meghan unlocked the door. She dropped her bags when she heard the phone ring.

"Hello."

"Meghan Eden?" She knew his voice.

"Yes," she calmly replied.

"It's Eric. Eric Nolan." The sound of his voice made her pulse race.

"Hi Eric," her mind raced with questions *Why was he calling? How did he get her number?*

11

"I'm sorry I missed our game this morning. I got called back in the middle of the night. There were complications on the set," he sounded sincere, but she wondered if it was the truth. She didn't want to trust anyone and especially someone from his world.

"That's okay. You would have lost anyway." She laughed. She thought it best to play it safe. She didn't want him to know what she really thought.

"I hope I can have the chance sometime to prove you wrong," he tossed at her.

"Maybe." She wondered if he meant it.

"At least you didn't say no. I am sorry. I didn't want to call in the middle of the night. I should have left a message at the front desk but I thought I would've had the chance to call you before now."

Meghan thought he sounded sincere. "How did you get my number?" she asked.

"I have an agent that will do anything. It will probably cost me, but you're worth every cent," he admitted. Meghan swallowed hard. *He wants me. Why?* She laughed, "You hardly know me".

"My mom always told me I would know when I met the right woman." His direct remark forced Meghan to sit down suddenly. She wasn't sure how to answer that one and fell silent.

"Still there or did I scare you away?" he asked.

"I'm still here," she responded.

"I just wanted to get away from my crazy world for a couple of days and a game of golf. Then I met you. Was it coincidence or fate?" he asked.

Meghan didn't respond. She wanted to tell him how she felt but she couldn't.

"Meg, when I looked into your eyes, I knew. When you didn't know who I was, it intrigued me. You made me feel human again. I'm just that ordinary guy you golfed with. I felt that something in our kiss. I can't get it out of my mind. It was unforgettable. If you didn't feel it, just tell me."

Her heartbeat increased when she heard him use the same word to describe the kiss. She found it hard to catch a breath. It sounded too good to be true. She wanted to believe him. She wanted to tell him she couldn't get that kiss out of her mind.

"Still there?" he asked quietly.

"Yes, I'm still here. I'm not sure what to say," she admitted.

"Is it okay if I call to talk?" he asked.

What harm can there be in talking? The sound of his voice, that kiss etched in her mind answered for her. "It's okay," she answered.

"So how's the phone sex with one of the most beautiful, desired men as *People* states?" Paige tossed a copy of the magazine on Meghan's desk.

"I'm not having phone sex Paige. And I don't read gossip." Meghan threw the magazine in her trash can and laughed.

"Yeah, right Meg. I haven't seen you smile like this, ever." Paige went back to her office and Meghan reached for the magazine. His face on the cover only took her memory back to that kiss. That damn kiss etched in her mind kept her contemplating her decision to never love again. Eric Nolan was definitely on her mind every day since Arizona. She loved their daily conversations, sometimes for hours and late into the night. Meghan knew she wasn't ready to share the complete details of her pain but she enjoyed being his friend. She shook her head and told herself to get back to work. First she shoved the magazine in her purse. She wanted to read it when she went home. More so, she wanted to have his picture.

Eric called her that night. She'd been reading the article.

"Hi Meg. How was your day?"

Oh I spent the day thinking about you. Reading the article in People and then wanting to be in your arms— your lips pressed against mine.

She smiled and shook those thoughts. "It was good. How was yours?" She wished she had the guts to tell him what she actually thought.

"Mine was good. I received the date for the movie premier in New York. I was hoping you would join me."

There was a pause. She feared she may have let him believe she could offer him more than friendship. She wanted more, but couldn't admit it. It scared her to think of the possibility.

"No pressure Meg. Think about it."

Meghan's defenses were up. The desperate desire to see him again, to be kissed by him was beginning to win, but she never wanted to lose again.

"I can't Eric. It's too soon." The hurt still ached deep within her heart and she refused his offer.

Meghan spent the next few days with regret. Eric called after the premier to share the details with her.

"I'm sorry I didn't go with you Eric." Eric brought a passion into her life she had never experienced, with just one kiss. To think beyond a kiss scared her.

"It's okay Meg. You're not ready. I won't pressure you."

She could never understand why this man was so patient with her. "One of these days you will stop calling me."

"That won't happen, Meg. I loved you from the moment I seen those eyes. I told you before if your friendship is all you can offer, I'm fine with that. Whenever you are ready, I'll be here."

Meghan felt something very powerful that made her heart beat faster and filled her with desire. She denied it was love. 'Love' was one word she swore she'd never use again.

"Meg?"

"I'm still here. I'm not being fair to you Eric. You should be with someone who can actually spend time with you," Meghan's eyes filled with tears. Her heart ached. She didn't want to keep him from having someone special to share his life with.

"I only want you Meg. Until you're ready, I have the chaotic film industry to keep me busy," he laughed. He always had a way to make her feel better. She laughed at his remark.

"What are you going to do now that you have time between movies?"

"I need this break. I don't have any plans but to be lazy on the beach with no one around, unless you want to join me?"

She'd never answered him before, terrified to give it a shot. But that kiss still burned in her memory. Her feelings for him had grown deeper. She knew she had to kiss him again.

"Will we be alone in Malibu?"

Unforgettable Kiss

Chapter Two

Whispering waves brushed along the beach. A gentle breeze feathered through Meghan's already tousled ash blonde hair. Her thoughts drifted to the life she once had. Meghan loved everything about the beach. It was the one place where she could forget her troubles and put her life into perspective. Changes in her life had taken her from one coast to another, but there was always a beach. But this beach was different—it scared her. It was 'his' beach.

She felt hesitant. It had been a long time since she had been with a man. She'd only made love to one man, her husband Ben. But Eric was a dream, leaving her heart open to possibility. She feared her heart overruled her strength. There was always that 'if.' She couldn't go through it all again. The loss, the pain that still ripped through her heart had almost convinced her not to come.

The phone call he had to take left her alone contemplating her decision. She was her own worst critic. She'd come to Malibu, but still struggled with her decision. No man had ever swept her off her feet—

not even her husband. No man had ever made her body tremble with a simple touch. She thought she'd loved her husband, but now she wondered if there had ever been passion. For that is what she felt with Eric; the heat in his presence, in his kiss. A kiss that was still so fresh in her mind, it filled her with such desire and made her heart ponderous. She could still taste him. She had breathed him all these weeks. She constantly tried to figure out the feelings that stirred within her. Here she was sitting on his beach, about to give her body and soul to him. What possessed her to come?

What's wrong with a little fun, Meghan? We both know you don't allow yourself to have any, ever. She chuckled to herself, remembering Paige's expression and the push she got at the airport gate. Paige always said what was on her mind, bluntly at times. She told Meghan there were no strings attached, no commitments to make; just a little wicked wild fun. Remembering Paige's words made her smile. But that was not Meghan Eden. Yet here she was, on his beach. She'd wandered off to the beach when he took the call. The ever-so-soft breeze gently caressed her face. She felt a warm touch on her shoulder. She turned to the most intriguing dark eyes of the handsome man who had drifted into her life.

"I thought I'd find you here," he spoke softly. The way his lips formed each word continued to mesmerize her every time. Meghan held her hand out to him. He put his hand into hers and pulled her gently to him. She felt desirable in his embrace. Eric found his way into Meghan's life; she wanted to let him into her heart. She felt his passion as he held her. His eyes locked onto hers.

"You have the most amazing eyes. They are more powerful and beautiful than any ocean. Yet, they are still so calming." Eric had told her many times he couldn't get them out of his mind. He gently placed his finger on her lips. "May I kiss you? I've wanted to do this again for the longest time," he smiled. She nodded. His lips met hers with a kiss so soft, but with such passion. The instant his lips moved slowly across hers, she forgot her thoughts of leaving. She felt as though she was in a safe comfort zone in his arms. His lips left hers and he whispered in her ear, "We have to get ready for dinner. Our guests will be here soon." Eric had invited a couple of his closest friends to meet her. She'd agreed to meet the friends he always spoke of. She also thought it would help ease her being there with him.

Meghan walked out onto the terrace. Eric stood, strikingly handsome. He had just poured a scotch and almost got it to his lips when he looked up. Meghan glided effortlessly toward him. His eyes never left her. His glass never made it to his lips. Her dress, in the palest of yellows, hugged every curve of her body. She heard him sigh and she smiled. The dress had been successful. She stood so close, she felt him take a hard quick breath. She wanted to taste his lips. She swallowed hard at his words.

"When you look at me, I see what I've been searching for."

She didn't know how to respond to his remark. She decided to give him a twirl as if he had meant the dress and not her. "Glad you approve."

Eric stumbled to get the words out. "Now how am I supposed to entertain dinner guests tonight with you distracting me?"

Meghan threw him a bashful grin and pulled his hips closer to her. It wasn't like her, but she desperately wanted this man. She needed to touch him. *What's wrong with a little fun?* She remembered Paige's words. She traced a finger down the side of his face. He easily succumbed to this erotic gesture. She surprised herself with her actions but at the same time didn't care. This time she wouldn't back out. The faint sound of the doorbell brought them back to reality.

"I want to meet your friends. We'll play later."

"Promise?"

Eric threw her a playful grin and placed the palm of his hand on her lower back. She took in a quick breath. The simple touch ignited a desire long hidden. The thought of his hands all over her body and his lips

21

passionately against hers; she knew it was going to be a long evening. The doorbell rang again. Eric smiled, "My friends are waiting. I want them to meet the woman who has stolen my heart". Eric opened the door to his best friends since college, Sandy and Nick. Sandy hugged Eric, "We've been dying to meet her".

She spotted Meghan. "It's great to meet you Meghan. I had to meet the woman who stole Eric's heart. He's never let anyone in." She embraced Meghan and introduced her husband Nick.

"Don't mind her Meghan. She's a little outspoken." Nick laughed.

"A little?" Eric added.

Sandy gave them an evil stare, "For that remark, I'm going to share all the dirt". She winked at Meghan. Meghan was comfortable and content with his friends. The evening was filled with great conversation and laughter. She closed the door after saying good night to his friends.

Eric stood for a moment and looked into her eyes "I hope you didn't forget your promise."

Meghan moved closer to him. Her fingers travelled through the silk of his jet black hair. One fingertip traced along the side of his face and she gently caressed the outline of his mouth.

"I never back out of a promise," she smiled.

She placed her hand on his chest, and the tempo of his pulse increased. She could feel herself tremble, getting weaker by the moment. Reality faded and paradise set in. He pulled her hips in closer to his. The passion she felt could defy analysis. Meghan told herself to react, not respond. He pushed her shoulders against the wall, aggressive yet gentle, with an incredible rhythm. His hips never left hers in the sudden movement. An insatiable appetite stirred within her. He stretched her arms up and slowly traced the contour of her body. His thumbs butted against her breasts along the way to her hip. His eyes locked onto hers. Her lips parted. She invited his kiss she could no longer resist. Quickly taking her, his tongue felt like silk as it slowly entered into the warm depths of her mouth. It was time to take this relationship to the next level. His hands moved from her waist to where the zipper on her dress began. He unzipped it to allow his hands to explore the soft skin up to the tips of her shoulders. She softly moaned.

"Open your mouth" he commanded and he kissed her again. Her body trembled as he pressed against her. She felt his arousal. No man ever touched her like this before. She felt inexperienced. Eric touched her in ways she had never dreamed of. She felt wanted, desired, and needed. Eric had all that and more. Meghan felt his heart beat faster against her as he slowly lifted her dress from her shoulders and let it drop to the floor. She suddenly felt shy. Her eyes dropped down to where her dress lay. He lifted her chin with one finger and her eyes met his.

"You are so beautiful."

Her body trembled. She wondered if he sensed her shyness. It was as if he could read her mind.

"Trust me." He caressed the curves of her face.

She stood and looked into his dark eyes not knowing what to say. She smiled. A little embarrassed, she spoke honestly, "I'm not sure what to…"

He stopped her, placing a finger on her lips.

"Don't worry. I'll show you. I want to teach you what passion can be all about. Trust me, Meg."

She nodded. Reality slipped away. At this moment she was happy to be desired. She was safe in his arms.

He shifted his body and her eyes briefly closed. She felt him hard against her body. He moved slowly from her mouth down the length of her neck. Her eyes opened. She watched him devour her inch by inch. His tongue stopped at the tip of her breast and she whimpered lightly. Eric swept her into his arms and carried her upstairs to the bedroom. He laid her on the bed and stood before her. He undressed and slipped into bed beside her.

He took her hand and guided it to his chest. She felt his heart pound. He led her hand down to feel his desire for her. One hand gently caressed her breast. The other barely touched her skin as it travelled to the top of her thigh. She sighed and arched her body with his touch. His eyes never left hers. His hands locked on hers above her head. She was his, completely. A trail of clothes had been left behind along the way. The rest of the world; forgotten.

The sounds of the beach woke her. The warm breeze gently caressed her face. Meghan opened her eyes and found Eric watching her.

"Morning," she spoke softly.

Eric smiled. "Actually, it's afternoon."

"What! What time is it? I can't believe I slept this long." Meghan exclaimed in a panic and jumped out of bed. Eric crawled over to her side of the bed and pulled her back in.

"And, where do you think you're going? He tickled her until they both laughed. Meghan tried to blurt out something about her shop while laughing until reality hit.

"Oh yeah, I'm on holiday. But I should still call in to check on things."

"No one is going anywhere." Eric pulled her over on top of him. She kissed him and reality drifted away again. One kiss and she sensed his arousal. No longer afraid, she let herself go as she kissed him. Softly at first, barely touching his lips but when his mouth opened, she followed his lead into a sensual experience. Bodies pressed against each other, hearts pounding; she whispered his name. Their eyes locked onto each other, passion burned. Meghan felt a sensational tingle throughout her entire being. A heavy sigh and she cried out his name. Eric held her tight in his strong arms as their bodies overcame an incredible pleasure. She had finally discovered passion. Exhausted, she lay her head back on the pillow beside his. He smiled.

It was another hour before they found their way to the shower. He washed her back, stroked her ever so slightly. She felt the strength in his hands. She moaned and arched her body up against his. She grasped at the shower wall and he held her waist and pulled her tighter against him. The shower trickled over them as excitement reached its highest point. There was a moment of silence before Meghan turned to him and suggested they put clothes on if they ever planned on getting out of the house.

Meghan had never left her business before. It was in its second year and thriving. Her partner Paige, and their team, were like family; she knew she could trust them. The shop was in good hands and they promised to call her if anything urgent came up that required her attention. They made her promise to enjoy her holiday that she so well deserved.

Eric suggested they take a drive up the coast. There was a remote little restaurant with a terrific ocean view. No one would know them—well, not Eric anyway. She liked being from a small town with a small profitable business. The scenic ride up the coast was relaxing for the exhausted lovers. A quiet dinner and time alone was what they needed. Meghan still felt as though she didn't belong in his world but as she looked at him across the table, she didn't care. She wanted to enjoy the moment— *their* moment. Right now, she didn't want to think of what the future held. She was a survivor and no longer made plans or commitments. Even with her business, she went month to month with her main focus on her clients on a day-to-day basis. The thought of love forever, or a perfect life, left a torn empty space in her heart. Their friendship had definitely taken a new path. Meghan still hadn't shared her past with Eric. He'd told her he would listen when she was ready to share. Someday she might let him in.

Meghan awoke early and looked at her phone at the bedside table. She'd missed a text message. She picked up her phone and read Paige's text, *Are you having some fun with that handsome man?* Meghan replied to her text with a simple, *Yes,* and a smiley face.

Meghan placed her phone back on the bedside table and felt Eric snuggle in close.

"You're awake early today," he said sleepily.

"Sorry, did I wake you?" She turned, gave him a tender kiss on the cheek and cuddled into him.

"You can wake me anytime." He flashed a playful grin which was rudely interrupted by the sound of the phone.

"This better be good," Eric said into the phone.

The conversation sounded like movie business, so she headed for the shower.

A half-hour later, Eric entered the kitchen and saw Meghan out on the terrace with her coffee. He grabbed a cup of coffee and joined her. He kissed her on the back of her neck and wrapped his arms around her waist. She turned to him. By the expression on his face, she suspected the call was bad news and she was right.

"Bad news?"

"My agent. The start date of the movie has been moved up a week."

"Disappointed?" he asked.

"A little, but I understand." She tried to give him a look of reassurance.

"How did I ever get so lucky to find you?" Eric touched her cheek ever so gently.

"I need another coffee," Meghan smiled. She wanted to avoid an intimate conversation and any discussion of emotions and feelings. She was a warm-hearted woman trying to put on a cold front.

"I need a shower," he kissed her on the forehead.

"When is the last flight out today?"

Eric walked into the kitchen and hung up the phone, "You don't have to change your flight. Stay. Enjoy the beach and your holiday."

Meghan didn't want to. This wasn't her home, her beach. It was his.

"I thought I'd head back just in case they need me. Two weeks is a long time to expect Paige to run everything."

He tenderly placed his hands on her face.

"They said they would call if they need you. Don't cut your time short because of me."

Meghan's honesty finally appeared. It was her nature. That's who she was.

"Well, you're not going to be here and I thought since this was your house—"

Eric cut her off, "Come on, Meg, you're not a guest here. I want you here. Haven't you yet realized how much I love you?" He gently kissed her forehead, holding her face in his hands.

"I want to be the face you see every morning. The touch you need every single night. I need you like the air that I breathe."

Oh no! She thought as she stared into his eyes. *This relationship has gone much farther than it should. What do I do? I want this man, I love. No. I can't do this again. It still hurts. I have to be stronger than this.*

A tear rolled down Meghan's cheek. Eric kissed it away.

"Please let me love you. I'll never leave you," he pleaded. Meghan turned so he would not see her cry.

"You can't promise that."

"Take the chance Meg. I know you feel it."

"I can't."

"If this isn't love we're making Meg, then what is it?"

She didn't reply. She walked out onto the terrace and down to the beach, her place of serenity. He watched her from the window stroll along the beach for a few minutes then went for a drive. When he returned she was gone. All that was left was a note on his pillow. His hand trembled as he reached for the note.

Eric, sorry for leaving like this but I think its best. I'm just not ready for a commitment. The loss, the hurt, I can't risk that again. No one can make a promise to never leave, to never hurt. I treasure the time we've spent. I will miss you. Passionate Kisses, Meg

The plane took off. She spoke to no one. She thought of her son and her husband who destroyed her world in one single moment. Meghan still blamed herself for making her husband spend time with his own son. *I should have never forced him to take little Ben to the ballgame that night. Why did he have to drink and drive with our son in the car?* Tears filled her eyes and ran down her cheeks. She had lost everything that night. Meghan walked away from her husband and never spoke to him again. She never even attended his sentencing to manslaughter. She swore she'd never love again.

Chapter Three

Meghan checked her voice mail after she unpacked. Her mom and a couple of business contacts left messages but she didn't really pay much attention, her mind was in another place. She opened the fridge but she had no appetite. Then she heard his voice and froze. She walked into the living room and plopped down on her white leather couch. - She replayed the message so many times she'd committed it to memory. Each time she still felt sad.

I just called to see if you made it back safely. I miss you Meg. I don't want to push you away, but I have to tell you how I feel. How you make me feel. I don't want to lose you. I understand. Call anytime.

She wanted to call him back. He sounded worried and heartbroken. *No. Don't do it Meg.* She sat for a long time staring out the window. The radio was on low. She heard the song, 'In the Air Tonight,' play in the background. Part of her wanted him but she hated playing with his heart. She knew there was no way she could commit to him. She couldn't love him. She couldn't bear another loss. Tears fell down her face as she tried to convince herself not to call him.

Meghan didn't sleep well and when the phone rang early in the morning, she remembered she hadn't returned her mother's call. Without looking, she pressed the 'Talk' button.

"I've woken you. I'm sorry." She knew that voice in an instant. She sat up quickly in bed, combing her hand through her hair.

"Hi Eric."

"Did you sleep well?"

"No. I didn't sleep much."

"Me either. I miss you Meg." His voice sounded shaky to her.

There was a pause. Meghan bit her lip. She didn't know what to say or how to say what she knew she should.

"Meg? If it's time you need, if we're moving too fast, whatever it is, whatever I can do—"

Meghan interrupted.

"Eric, don't do this. It's not you or time I need. It's me. I don't want to string you along because I can't commit or even say the "L" word. You don't deserve that. You are too good of a person."

"Meg, you are a good person too. You're not stringing me along. It's okay not to say the "L" word." He chuckled and Meghan laughed.

"I guess calling it the "L" word sounds a little funny. We're not kids. But see, I can't even say it. Eric, you've given so much and I can't."

"Meg, you've given me more than you'll ever know. You don't have to say anything you're not ready to. I truly understand. Call anytime. I'm here for you. I miss you Meg."

"What have I done? See the damage I already created? Eric, I have to go."

"Okay. Just remember you can call anytime. I'm here for you. I miss you Meg."

Meghan hung up the phone as tears ran down her cheeks. She spent the rest of the day in bed thinking of him, aching for him. She'd denied herself what he had to offer. She whispered through a cry: *He's a wonderful passionate man who loves me and I can't let him in.* Meghan picked up little Ben's picture that she kept on her nightstand. It was the only picture she left of her little boy. She had packed the rest away. She remembered the love she had for her son, and her prayers that his father would love him too. It still hurt. *How can I love again?* She cried herself to sleep.

Meghan woke at nine o'clock that night starving. She hadn't eaten in two days. She needed food and a shoulder to cry on.

Meghan picked up the phone and called Paige.

"Where are you?" Paige asked.

"I'm home. I need food and a good friend."

Paige arrived twenty minutes later with a pizza and a bottle of wine. "Meg, when did you get back? And why?" Meghan told Paige everything.

"Meg, what are you doing? You have a man that loves you, adores you and wants you. What are you so afraid of? Losing again? You can't assume that will happen. If it does, then you'll get through it."

Meghan knew she was right. Her thoughts drifted back to Arizona and the day she met Eric on the golf course. She remembered his voice, his intriguing dark eyes and his sweetness. No one had ever grabbed her attention the way he had. There was definitely electricity when their hands touched and something oddly familiar as if they had known each other before. Those few hours on the course were competitive, but fun. She had never felt so comfortable with someone. They'd laughed over dinner about the fact that she hadn't a clue who he was. She'd apologized, but he said he liked it better being that 'ordinary guy.' There was definitely an attraction. Then there was that kiss. The kiss that burned her memory for months; the one that finally made her give in and go to Malibu. It was only three months ago, but it seemed like a lifetime. Lost in her thoughts, she didn't hear a word Paige was said.

"Paige, it's not fair to lead this man into a relationship that I cannot commit to."

"Meghan, you are in love with this man. If you weren't, you wouldn't cry on my shoulder."

"What if—"

"Stop it Meg. You can't live your life with 'what-ifs.' Don't walk away from this second chance at happiness."

"You're probably right, but I'm scared." Meghan opened up the pizza box.

"I'm always right." Paige smiled and poured the wine.

Meghan woke up early the next morning. She had dreamed of Eric. She decided to take the advice of her best friend. She reached for the phone and dialed his number. He picked up before the second ring.

"Has anyone ever told you how sexy you sound on the phone?"

"Meg?"

"I'm sorry. I've been a coward," she said.

"No you haven't Meg. I'm a very patient man. I've waited my whole life for you. I wish I wasn't on set and we had more time to spend together, but I will call every free minute I can," he promised.

"Paige says we're having phone scx," she said and laughed.

"Now you're giving me ideas. I'll have to find a very private place for that chat," he laughed.

"I'm being paged. I promise to call when I get a chance."

"And, Meg, I'm happy you called.

"Me too," she smiled and pressed End Call.

Paige was already at the shop when Meghan arrived.

"Well, I can tell by the look on your face, you took my advice."

"Yes, I did. I called Eric this morning."

"And?"

Meghan smiled and walked toward her office, "He still wants me".

Meghan attempted to bury herself in the mound of paperwork on her desk and return phone calls. She couldn't focus, her mind kept dreaming of that night in Malibu in Eric's arms. Paige walked past her office a few times but said nothing. The one time Paige did interrupt her was when Eric called. Paige stuck her head into Meghan's office.

"Mr. Right is on line three, babe." Meghan smiled and Paige closed her door.

She picked up the phone and in her most professional voice, said, "Meghan Eden."

"Do I still sound sexy to you?" he asked. That simple raspy tone made her smile.

"Mr. Nolan, I didn't expect to hear from you so soon."

"Get used to it. I'm not letting you get away again."

For the next three months he called every day and every night. She missed him terribly and fantasized about his touch every night. Meghan thought three months would be a lifetime without his touch but she was so busy with the wedding season that she didn't even visit her mom. She attended a conference in Boston and another in Long Island for new Spa products. She would have loved a quick detour to visit her mom since the conferences were on the east coast, but there wasn't time in between and she needed to get back. She didn't want to leave Paige alone during their busiest season.

Meghan made it back for the July Fourth barbecue at Paige's cottage. She hadn't been there since her son's death. It was too close to her cottage. Meghan couldn't go there without her son but didn't have the heart to sell it. She treasured the memories spent with her son. Her husband never went with them. He was too occupied with his climb to partnership in the investment firm.

"Dreaming of Mr. Right?" Paige threw her arms around Meghan, which startled her. She knew she could never lie to Paige. Paige had tried to set her up a couple of times with unattached lawyers at her husband's firm but Meghan always told her she wasn't ready. She was unsure she was ready for Eric.

"You caught me. But, I don't know if we should call him Mr. Right."

"I wish you would admit it Meg," Paige laughed.

"Maybe after a drink."

"This way, my friend," Paige led them to the deck and her private stash.

The celebration went late into the night with fireworks and a lot of wine, and afterward, Paige sent her home in a cab.

For the first time Meghan dragged herself into the shop at noon the next day.

"I see we're a little under the weather today,'" Paige remarked sarcastically.

"Just a little. Sorry I'm so late," Meghan replied and headed for her office.

"What powerful potion did you feed me last night, Paige?"

Paige laughed, "Ancient family secret."

Meghan tried to laugh, but it hurt too much. Paige was ready with a glass of water in one hand and aspirin in the other. Meghan took the aspirin.

"Eric called twice this morning," Paige mentioned and took the empty glass from Meghan's hand.

"Yeah, he left a message this morning. I didn't have the strength to answer the phone." Meghan could barely speak.

"If you think you are strong enough now to hold down the fort..." Paige started and Meghan motioned it was okay. "Is Michael going to make it to lunch this time?" Paige had told her he had missed the last few lunch dates and she ended up having lunch with his staff. "Hope so," Paige sighed.

Meghan accomplished nothing while Paige was out. She watched Paige enter the door and wondered how she could be so energetic when they drank the same amount.

"Oh Meg, you don't look good."

"I don't feel good."

"You're at the right place to make you feel better," Paige suggested a massage. Meghan looked at her reflection in the mirror, "Good idea. I look horrible".

"Your many fans from the law firm think differently. They were impressed with that little red sundress." Paige winked at her. "They were still talking about you babe, over lunch." Paige raised an eyebrow.

Meghan just rolled her eyes. "They should see me today." She and Paige laughed. Paige motioned her toward the spa treatment room. Eric called again.

"Paige, I'm worried Meg has disappeared from my life again."

"I assure you Eric she hasn't. Meghan is still very much in love with you even though she won't admit it to you, me or herself for that matter." Paige laughed.

"Thanks Paige. I hope you're right."

"I'm always right. We had a few drinks last night at my Fourth of July party. Meg is having a massage as we speak, and then I'm shipping her home to bed."

"Thanks for the idea, Paige. I need your help to surprise Meg," Eric said.

"Sure. Anything for my best friend."

Meghan left for home feeling rejuvenated. She stopped at the grocery store for some remedies to cure her hangover. She took her grocery bag into the kitchen and checked her phone messages.

"Oh shit, Mom! I'm sorry, I forgot to call again," she said aloud. She was used to talking to herself; she lived alone. Suddenly she heard laughter coming from the bedroom. She knew that laugh but what was he doing here? Quickly she ran down the hall.

"Eric? When did you get here?" She felt so excited to see him. He was waiting in her bed and from what she could tell, he had nothing on but a smile on his face and a single red rose between his teeth.

He handed the rose to her. "We finished early. I thought I'd surprise you. Paige gave me a key. You're not mad are you?"

"Heavens no, what a wonderful surprise, I've missed you." Meghan ran her fingers through his hair and down his jawline until she reached the lips she desired.

He pulled her closer to him. Months of wanting and needing exploded. He unbuttoned her blouse. His strong hands roamed over her breasts and then up to her shoulders and removed her blouse slowly down her arms. His lips found that soft spot along the side of her neck. He stroked her thighs. Her body moved with his every touch. She could no longer resist. He inched his way back to those soft lips. His eyes locked onto her blues. There was hunger in his eyes.

"I want you," she whispered against his lips. She no longer cared, no longer shied away from him. In one quick sudden movement, he tossed her underneath him.

"I want you Meg. I've never wanted another woman the way I want you." His lips caressed every curve of her face and then met her lips. Passion grew stronger. His tongue travelled along the curve of her body. She felt his tongue capture the moistened heat between her thighs. Her body arched and moved with every touch until it brought her to the point of no return. She heard his soft throaty moans as he entered. She pulled her thighs up and hard against him. His hands grasped her hair and she held him tight at his waist. Meghan felt unbelievable desire and cried out his name. Her debilitated body lay intertwined with Eric's. She drifted into sleep in his arms.

Meghan phoned Paige the next morning, "Morning Paige. Can you mind the shop on your own today?"

"Are you still feeling hung?" Paige sounded concerned.

"Uh ...no ...I'm fine, uh ..." Meghan laughed and disconnected the call.

Chapter Four

Paige turned to her husband, who was just waking, "Why don't we ever spend the day in bed?"

Michael got out of bed and headed for the shower, "Some of us are responsible with our businesses."

His answer was cold. Paige wondered how many years they'd been married. She shrugged it off and headed for the kitchen. She waited for the coffee to brew and thought back to the beginning of their relationship. Their passion was spontaneous. She hadn't thought about it in a while. She wondered if maybe she'd drifted away from him as well. She couldn't remember the last time they were actually intimate. Not since the miscarriage? Michael came up behind her and reached his arm around her.

"Getting fresh this morning, darling?" Paige hoped.

"You're standing in front of the coffee pot. Better snap out of whatever it is you're thinking about. You have a business to run yourself, remember? "Michael remarked, more like her father and not her husband. Before she knew it, he was out the door and left her standing there without even a kiss goodbye.

Paige wondered what happened to their passion. They had always had it. They were so in love. *Were? What happened? It can't be gone.* Michael hadn't paid much attention to her in months and lately he seemed so cold with his remarks on, well, on everything she spoke about. They were both so wrapped up in their careers since the miscarriage; they hadn't noticed that their marriage suffered. They had been distant for months, since their discussion, which turned into an argument. Paige wanted to discuss their options for having a baby. Michael's quick rejection of adoption stopped the discussion.

Paige's thoughts drifted back to the night they first realized they were in love. She had been the Office Administrator at his law firm. She became his friend when his wife left him to move back to England. He confided in Paige that he was devastated. He told her he had been faithful and loyal to his wife for the twenty-seven years they'd been married. He'd truly adored his wife, Liz and their daughter Tonia. Tonia was now twenty-six and also living in England. Michael was left all alone and confessed to Paige it was difficult to go on. He spent endless hours burying himself in his work. Paige's heart went out to him. He was a handsome man, so gentle and kind. At forty-seven, he had a thriving law firm. Everyone in the firm adored him. Paige told him there were many women interested since he was now available. He told Paige he was in great emotional pain and not interested. Paige had been there for him as his friend.

She remembered that late night at the office. It was after eight o'clock when she was getting ready to leave and noticed his office light still on. She knocked on his door and he quietly said to come in. Paige gently opened the door and saw something she had never noticed before. A strikingly handsome man, strong features, sparkling emerald green eyes, and the five o'clock shadow of stubble on his face that only brought out his manliness. His thick black hair, usually groomed, was messed up and gave him a sexy look. He looked up at her and she melted. A strong desire sizzled through every vein in her body.

He spoke in a tired raspy voice, it appealed to her. Paige stuttered a bit, still shocked at the thoughts that had just passed through her mind.

"I was just about to lock up and noticed your lights still on."

"Too hard to go home to an empty house." He smiled out of the corner of his mouth, "What are you still doing here on a Friday night? Shouldn't you be out on a hot date?"

Paige smiled at him. "Well, you know, so many offers, I couldn't decide," she said and he laughed along with her.

"Young, beautiful and hard-working, what a pity. Some man doesn't know what he's missing."

His remark hit her hard. She figured he was joking with her. Her long auburn hair had fallen out of its neatly kept French twist and hung around her face.

"I'm sure I still look my best," she sarcastically remarked. They were good friends who were both outspoken and could say anything to each other. She was the one person he had opened his heart to and his grief. He smiled again. He looked lost in his thoughts. She wondered what he had been thinking. "What's on your mind to make you smile?" Paige asked and walked toward his desk. She plumped herself down in the chair in front of his desk. Her long slender legs stretched out in front of her. She noticed his attention drifted to her legs.

"Michael?" Paige asked again and he looked up. He began to focus on gathering up the papers in front of him. He looked a little flushed in the face. She wondered what he'd been thinking.

"You wouldn't want me to tell you what I've just been thinking," he finally answered her.

She crossed one leg over the other. She watched his eyes as this simple movement brought his attention

47

back to her legs. She sensed she was making him uncomfortable.

"You can tell me anything Michael, you know that," she said, flirting with him.

"Yes, I do know. I think I've been working too long today. I'm starting to think of you in ways I shouldn't be," he confessed.

"Oh? Now I'm definitely intrigued," Paige said with a slight laugh.

Michael laughed and blushed.

"You're blushing. Are you having naughty thoughts of me?" She walked around his desk to him, and sat on the comer of his desk, just inches away from him. He eased back into his chair and smiled at her. "So, Mr. Adams, exactly how have you been picturing me and where?" she asked, playing with him.

He pulled her onto his lap and brushed her hair away from her face. There was a moment of silence as their eyes met. Suddenly their lips met and he kissed her. The hunger she felt caught her off guard. She never imagined she could feel this way. She ached for more when their lips parted. He finally answered her question, "In my bed."

Still overwhelmed from the kiss and slowly coming back to reality,   she asked, "What?"

"You asked me where I pictured you and I answered."

For the first time, someone shocked Paige. "How did this happen?"

He softly caressed the side of her face. "I don't know, but it feels right, to me anyway."

"It feels right to me too." She kissed him again.

"Come home with me Paige," he pleaded.

Their night of passion was unbelievable. From that night on they'd never been apart. They were married six months later. When she told him she wanted to open the Spa with Meghan, he supported her completely.

For the past year though, he'd been distant. They grieved separately instead of together after the miscarriage of an unplanned pregnancy. She knew Michael's true feelings about any more children in his life at his age. She'd accepted it in the beginning. After the feeling of having a baby inside her—his baby— she yearned to have a baby. But the miscarriage created complications and Paige would never be able to conceive again. She tried to discuss adoption, but he shut her out. The matter was never discussed after that night of hurtful remarks. They both hid their feelings through their work. Now Paige finally realized it wasn't the passion that was missing; it was the fact they never dealt with the matter. She felt lonely even with him there.

Angela Ford

Chapter Five

"What? Oh my God! When?" Eric heard Meg's hysterical words as he walked into the kitchen. He immediately went to her and put his arm around her. She was on the phone, crying. He could barely understand what she was saying and only heard one side of the conversation. He heard her say that she'd be there as soon as she could. Meghan ended the call and turned into Eric's open arms. Deep breaths and gasping cries were all he heard.

"What happened," he asked and held her tight.

"My mom had a stroke. She's in intensive care. They don't think she'll make it. I have to get to her."

Eric wasn't sure what to do. He tried to console her as much as he could every time she ran to him for comfort. She tried to throw some things into a suitcase. He was at a loss for words. All he could do was comfort her through his embrace.

Eric drove her to the airport and held her in his arms as they said goodbye. Meghan uttered that she forgot to call Paige, and as he brushed her hair away from her face, and kissed her forehead, he promised he'd go right to the shop to tell her. Without another word or touch, she was once again gone.

When Eric arrived at the shop, he found Paige on the phone. He must have looked impatient for her to finish the call, because she quickly ended it with a look of great concern on her face. Eric told her about Meghan's mom.

"Oh no! Is she okay?" Paige blurted out the words without a breath and tears streamed from her eyes.

"All I know is that her mom had a stroke and is in Intensive Care and Meg said they told her it didn't look good."

Meghan phoned Paige the next day to let her know she'd made it home.

"Meg, I'm so sorry, how are you holding up?" Meghan began to cry again.

"Paige, why did this happen to her? She's always been so healthy?"

"How is your mom?" Paige did not want to ask if she had died.

Through sobbing tears, Meghan responded to her friend. "Oh, Paige, I did make it home, but only for a few minutes and then...and then she was gone. I was holding her hand. She looked so peaceful."

"Meg, I can be there tomorrow if you want," Paige offered.

"Thanks Paige. I'll be okay. I need you to hold things up at that end." Meghan was grateful Paige was there for the business.

Meghan had one more call to make, to Eric.

"Eric. I'm sorry I haven't called."

"How's your mom?" he asked.

"She's gone." Meghan started to cry.

"Meg, do you want me to come?"

She gained her composure and took a deep breath. "No. I need this time with my family and sort through this Eric. I'm feeling guilty. I promised to visit my mom a few times and didn't. I was wrapped up in my business. Then you. I need some time." Meghan had once again put the walls up around her heart.

"I understand. I'm here if you need me Meg. I love you."

There was no reply. Just dial tone

Eric took a flight back to Malibu.

****

Paige was sitting on the back deck that evening when Michael arrived home from a long day in court.

"Here you are. Hiding?" he laughed, until he saw the look on Paige's face. Paige looked up at him solemnly. "Meg's mom had a stroke and didn't make it."

"Oh. And that leaves you to run the business alone?"

Paige looked at him furiously and stormed past him. She spent the rest of the evening upstairs. When she heard him come up the stairs, she rolled over and pretended to be asleep. He never said a word. The next morning he had left for the office before Paige awoke. The coffee was on but no note. *Does he even think of me?* She wondered. *What has become of him?* Paige felt as though she didn't exist in his world.

Paige called Michael later that morning from the shop but he had already left for court. Tammy, his secretary, told Paige he wasn't expected back unit late afternoon and then offered to have lunch with Paige. Lately, Paige seemed to be having lunch more with Tammy then her husband. Paige thanked her and asked if they could meet at their usual spot about one o'clock. *I can't even get a lunch date with him.* Paige cursed under her breath as she hung up the phone.

Michael didn't arrive home that night until after nine. Paige was already in bed, reading. This time she didn't roll over and pretend to be asleep. She wanted and needed to spend time with her husband. He faintly smiled and nodded, then headed for the shower. He pecked her on the cheek as he crawled into bed and turned over.

"Have you eaten?" she asked.

"Yeah, after court with the guys," he mumbled without turning back.

"Hon," Paige said as she wrapped her arms around him and cuddled into him, "I think we need to get away, just the two of us."

"Not now. Maybe after the trial. Anyway, you've got the shop to run single-handedly."

"Well, when Meg gets back and the trial is over?" she asked.

"Sure, why not?" Within seconds he was snoring.

Paige turned out her light. She lay there hoping things would turn around. They both needed to rekindle what seemed to be burning out.

A week later, the shop door opened and there stood Meghan.

"Oh, Meg, I'm so sorry about your mom." Paige ran to her friend and embraced her in a hug.

"Thanks babe, it's been tough. How's everything here?" Meghan changed the subject. Paige accepted her friend's comment. She knew Meghan better than anyone when it came to loss. Paige knew Meghan would begin to bury herself in work again and that she simply didn't want to cry anymore. Paige respected her friend's wishes. Her heart went out to her. Meghan looked emotionally exhausted. Paige filled her in on the business. Things were booming with the wedding season.

"Oh, Paige, I forgot about the wedding bookings. You must be working day and night. Is Michael ready to kill me," Meghan asked.

"Well actually, no. He doesn't seem to have the time of day for me lately. I can't even get a lunch date," she said with a sarcastic tone of voice. She quickly took her focus back to the papers in front of her, hoping Meghan wouldn't see the tears that formed in her eyes.

"Yeah right. Since when?" Paige remained quiet.

"Paige? What's happening?"

Paige wiped away the tears on her cheeks and grasped tightly onto Meghan's extended hand. "My intuition tells me my marriage is in distress but you are the one suffering."

Meghan heard the anguish in Paige's voice. "Paige, I'm always here for you, as you are for me. Now tell me what happened? What intuition?"

Paige poured her heart out about late nights, no time for lunch dates and Michael's cold remarks. She told Meghan she couldn't remember the last time they were intimate. Meghan tried to reassure her friend that it was the court case. It was a long battle for Michael and that's what made him act like that. Meghan got up and went around to Paige to hug her.

"Oh, honey, I'm sorry I've been so wrapped up in my own life. You and Michael need to get away, just the two of you."

Paige's cries calmed and she told Meghan that she had already mentioned that to her husband and he replied "maybe," then rolled over and went to sleep. Meghan reached for the phone and handed it to Paige.

"Well. You know what you have to do. Don't get soft on me now. You know I need your strength." Meghan gave her the raised eyebrow, which was their signal for 'don't argue with me.' "Plan this romantic getaway now and don't take no for an answer," Meghan commanded.

"What would I do without you Meg?"

"No, it's more like, what would I do without you?" Meghan closed the door to Paige's office and left her alone to make those plans.

Chapter Six

Meghan felt emotionally exhausted. She had taken the red-eye flight back, and gone straight to work at the Spa for the day. Now home, she decided to pour herself a glass of wine and take a bath. Her emotions had been in overdrive of late. When she listened to her phone messages, there was a call from her dad making sure she got home safely.

He was so sweet, still worrying about her. She should be worrying about him. She knew her father had always been a strong man, but she worried her mother's passing would be his breaking point. He was her tower of strength at little Ben's funeral. This time it was different. He had lost his wife, his best friend. She remembered the night of the funeral when she couldn't sleep and got up to get a glass of water. She heard him in the dark, crying. At first she wanted to go and comfort him. She decided to give him the privacy he deserved and went back to her room. Meghan knew he needed time to deal with his loss. Not that time helped. Meghan still fought her loss. A single tear fell upon her cheek. Sadness she felt, tears she fought.

All you need is time. Her support group had tried so many times to tell her that. She had never put the pieces of herself back together to completely move forward. *Life does go on for those who are left behind,* the group also told her. It began to make sense. She also remembered the last words her dad said before she boarded the plane. *Remember Meggie, second-first chances don't come around often.* He had always called her Meggie. Meghan smiled at the thought of his words and the great man she always adored and respected.

Lost in thought, she forgot to save or delete the message. She replayed her messages. The next one stopped her thoughts completely just hearing the voice. *Meg, its Eric, I'm so sorry for the loss of your mom. I wish I could be there for you, but I won't push. Call anytime you want. I love you.* She played it over and over again. She thought of his touch, of his kiss. Then guilt set in; the guilt of spending the time with him and not with her mom like she had promised more than once. Now her mom was gone. Tears piled down her cheeks. She wished she had one more chance to spend time with her mom. She fought the tears; the same kind of tears she had fought when she lost her child.

How can one think of second-first chances Dad? I keep losing the ones I love.

She awoke the next morning with regret. She had not called her dad back. She reached for her phone.

"Oh Dad, I'm sorry, I forgot to call when I got back yesterday. Then last night when I got your message, I got lost in my own thoughts. I don't know where my mind is. Well, actually I do. Eric left a message too. I started thinking about Mom and how I planned to visit." She gasped for a breath and her dad didn't say anything. "I started to feel guilty about being wrapped up in my own life and forgetting Mom and—" Meghan began to cry and couldn't continue.

"Meggie, don't punish yourself. Remember what I told you about second-first chances?"

Meghan managed to utter through her sobs, "But, Dad, I feel like I forgot about Mom and now she's gone."

"Meggie, what happened with your mom was so sudden. None of us ever dreamed it would happen. We must remember the good times and keep those memories alive. Meggie, what I told you about second-first chances? That advice came from your mom. It was her wish you would find happiness and true love. That is what she wanted for you. And I do too."

"Oh, Dad, I'm sorry. Here I am rambling on and you are suffering too." More guilt settled inside Meghan.

"Don't worry about your old dad, Meggie. Your mom is always with me, always in my heart. You have to stop feeling guilty. Stop carrying so much on your shoulders. Now I want you to pull yourself together and call that man. Don't lose out on this chance that you've been given. Do this for your mother and for me, but most of all do it for you."

"I love you Dad"

"I love you too Meggie, always." His reassurance and strength were all that she needed.

Meghan went into the kitchen and started the coffee before she jumped into the shower. Feeling refreshed, she remembered her dad's wise words. She picked up the phone to call Eric. Once more she was ready to apologize, to try again. She hoped he was still that patient man. When there was no answer, she was reluctant to leave a message and pressed the End button. She did love him and was ready to admit it, if it wasn't too late.

Meghan and Paige arrived at the shop simultaneously. After they'd parked their cars, they hugged and walked toward the shop. Meghan unlocked the door.

"Hit the lights Meg and I'll start the coffee," Paige remarked as she followed Meghan in.

"Yeah, we both look like we could use it," Meghan sighed.

With two coffees in hand, Paige joined Meghan on the leather couch in the waiting area of their spa. "So what prevented your sleep?"

Meghan took her coffee and after a sip, felt the effects of its warmth. "Eric left a message. I must have listened to it a hundred times. Then I forgot to call my dad back. Then the rest of my night went to hell."

"You didn't call Eric back?"

"No."

"And, why not?"

Meghan set her coffee down and put her head into her hands. "I don't know. I was so excited to hear his voice. Then I started thinking of Mom and felt guilty about spending time with Eric when I should have visited her."

Paige put her arms around Meghan.

"Oh, honey, don't beat yourself up on this. What happened with your mom was so unexpected and terrible. You know your mom was happy Eric came into your life. She wanted this for you. She'd kick your ass right now for doing this to yourself."

Meghan laughed through tears. "Yeah, she would, wouldn't she?"

Paige wiped away Meghan's tears and smiled at her dear friend. "You bet! And if you don't pull yourself together, I'm going to have to do it for her!"

"My dad said so too," Meghan smiled. She knew her dad and Paige were right. The two were so alike and so strong.

Paige raised her eyebrow with her *I'm always right* look. Meghan had seen the look often enough to know what it meant.

"So, I take it you called your dad back?"

"This morning to apologize. He pretty much told me the same as you just did."

"So you know what you have to do?" Paige handed her the phone.

Paige started to walk away when Meghan asked, "What about your sleepless night?"

Paige continued to walk. "After you make that call."

That was Paige—selfless. Meghan smiled and took the advice of her friend and her dad and dialed Eric's number. There was no answer again and this time she started to leave a message. All she got out was "Eric —" when she heard a reply.

"Yes? Right behind you."

She knew that sexy and calming voice and turned. He stood in the doorway. She ran to him and threw her arms around him. "Eric, I was just about to leave you a message."

He didn't say anything, but kissed her passionately. It felt like heaven.

Paige entered the lobby of the shop. "Well, I see the phone call went well," she said with a sarcastic chuckle.

Meghan and Eric turned to her and smiled. "Yes, and I suggest you take your own advice," Meghan told her.

Paige waved at them and walked into her office, "Yeah...I think I will."

Meghan met Eric's eyes. He leaned into her. Once his lips met hers, she knew she was exactly where she wanted to be.

Paige was on the phone with her travel agent when Meghan walked into her office, smiling. Paige thanked the travel agent and hung up the phone.

"Now, I see I'm not the only one happy here"

"I just can't stop smiling, Paige. I never thought I'd ever feel this happy again. So are you making plans for a romantic getaway with that husband of yours?"

"Yep, all done. I'm going to surprise Michael tonight. The trial ends today, hopefully with good news." Paige needed and wanted her husband back and she was determined to make it happen." So, where's Eric? Meg, you didn't send him away again?" She raised her eyebrow and Meghan laughed.

"No. He flew from New York and he's exhausted, so I sent him to my place to catch some sleep."

"And I'm assuming you'll be heading home for a long lunch?"

"Perhaps." Meghan smiled, knowing damn well she would be.

Chapter Seven

A trail of rose petals led her down the hall. *I take it he's not sleeping.* She was right. He waited in bed for her, with the 'bubbly' on ice and a red rose. Lit candles filled the room.

"Is this all for me?"

"And there's more waiting for you." His teasing smile made her smile with anticipation. She sat on the bed next to him. No more words were spoken. There was no need. Passion overcame them instantaneously. He started to remove her clothes, his lips never parting hers. His hands powerfully explored as pieces of clothing were tossed to the floor. He swiftly changed the direction of his lips from her mouth to her bare breasts. His tongue taunted her hardened tips. Meghan lost all grasp of reality and she didn't care. Eric was all she needed. She no longer wanted to battle the emotions that once stopped her. She whispered his name in delight and reached for the button on her pants. He stopped her.

"Not yet. I need to enjoy you."

She did not respond. She looked deeply into his dark, piercing eyes. She swore she could feel his soul.

He smiled. Her body arched. "You drive me crazy," he said and buried his face beneath her hair. She could feel him breathe in her scent at the back of her neck. Her hunger for him grew stronger. A simple reassurance of her acceptance of his love only intensified the desire she felt for him.

She fell into ecstasy with his every touch, his every kiss. Meghan never dreamed she could ever feel this desired. Here he was. He had become her reality. His magical touch brought a spell upon her. She caressed his face slowly. With one finger, she traced through the soft hair on his chest. His chest felt so strong, so powerful. She gently passed over his nipples while he moaned and his body twitched. Her hands moved farther for his arousal. His body shifted to move with her hand. Her lips left his and travelled along his neckline down to his chest. The tip of her tongue grazed over his nipple and he cried out her name. He picked her up and tossed her beneath him.

The sudden dominant but tender act only heightened Meghan's hunger for him. His eyes never left hers in the sudden movement. He finished undressing her. His lips met hers in a passionate kiss and never parted until they reached that point of no return. He whispered in her ear, "I love you Meg."

There was no response. She thought she was ready to say it. She wondered if she was still fighting her fear of commitment. She did love him. She just couldn't say it out loud. Eric remained patient. Silence continued until her phone rang.

"Paige, what's wrong?" Meghan asked with concern in her tone and quickly sat up in bed.

Meghan walked out of the bedroom. Eric followed her.

"England. Why?" Meghan asked and turned to see Eric behind her with a look of concern. She touched him gently and gave him a look to reassure him. He took a deep breath. Meghan put her hand over the phone and whispered to him that Paige's husband took off to England. The look on his face said enough and she watched him walk out of the kitchen. She loved how he respected her friendship with Paige. She hadn't been able to completely confide in Eric but she'd told him Paige had been there for her when she lost her son. Meghan owed everything to Paige. Her best friend helped her through the toughest time in her life.

Eric gave Meghan some space and time to talk. She found him in the bedroom. She rambled as she searched for clothes. He walked over to her and placed his hands on her shoulders. "Take a deep breath. What happened?"

His voice, his simple touch calmed her enough to fill him in. She placed her hands on his face and kissed him. *This man is so understanding, so good to me. Why can't I tell him I love him?*

"Paige surprised Michael with a romantic getaway. They've been distant for some time. Probably due to the long drawn-out trial he's been dealing with. Before Paige could get a reaction from her surprise trip, he said he was leaving for England because his adult daughter needed him. She broke up with another boyfriend or something like that. It doesn't make any sense. Paige is devastated. I have to go to her."
She kissed him again and he smiled. "I have to go over there, she's a mess. Do you understand?"

Eric looked a little confused trying to piece together what was happening. "Yes, of course. You'd better go. It sounds as though she needs you and she's always been there for you." He kissed her and she turned to leave. Then she suddenly ran back to him and threw her arms around him and thanked him for understanding.

"I'm sorry, but she's my best friend and is always there for me and—"

Eric interrupted her as he held her tight in his arms, "Sweet, it is okay. She needs you. One of the reasons I love you so is because you care so genuinely." He kissed her once more before she left.

The two women embraced at Paige's door. "Oh, Meg, I'm okay. This is silly. You should be with Eric".

Meghan took off her coat and walked toward Paige's kitchen. "And miss out on pizza and wine with my best pal? Come on!"

Paige laughed and asked Meghan, "Why do we always do this?"

"What? Cry on each other's shoulders? Or pig out on pizza and drink wine?" Meghan continued to open the wine.

"Both."

"Cause we are hopeless saps?" Meghan smiled, and then asked Paige, "Did you order the pizza?" Her friend gave her a 'thumbs-up'.

Meghan met Paige on the back porch and handed her a glass of wine then sat beside her on the porch swing and reached for her friend's hand. She sensed Paige's hurt and frustration. Paige rested her head on Meghan's shoulder and the two sat quietly without a word for the next few minutes before Meghan broke the silence.

"Paige, honey, I hate to see you like this." She didn't know what else to say.

"I don't know what to think, Meg. I've tried. Maybe I'm too late. I understand the trial occupied most of his time but we've been through trials before that consumed his thoughts, his energy. This time it seems different. He's so distant."

Meghan knew Paige was right. Many trials consumed Michael over the years but he always shared his views with Paige and respected her input with his opening and closing remarks. After all, Paige worked with him for years and not only listened but understood. This trial was no different than the others. Meghan wondered why Michael was hiding from the woman he adored and loved dearly. Questions raced through Meghan's mind and she knew damn well they raced through Paige's.

The faint sound of the doorbell blocked those thoughts. Meghan got up to answer the door and came back seconds later with a pizza. She tried to get Paige to eat something with no luck. She hardly even touched her wine. Paige sat there with an empty look. It was time for Meghan to step in and she knew just what she had needed to do. She excused herself to make a phone call.

"Hello"

"Michael? It's Meg. Do you have time to talk?"

"Meg, Is everything okay?"

He sounded concerned. Meghan would usually never call him on his cell. She knew he would have landed by now. "'Not really. Why did you take off to England when your wife needs you? What is going on between you two?"

"Tonia needs me." His short response told Meghan he didn't want to talk. His tone told her he had given a lame excuse. She wasn't going to let him off easy.

"You haven't seen or heard from your daughter since she went to England with her mother. Why all of a sudden are you running to her? Tell me the truth Michael. Please, for Paige's sake. She's devastated thinking the marriage is over."

Michael sighed without giving any explanation.

"Michael?"

"I'm here."

"I guess I'm not getting any answers."

Meghan was frustrated and ready to hang up.

"Wait, Meg, I know how much you care for Paige, and I do too. The trial has been consuming but it's not just that." Meghan was relieved he was ready to open up. One of them had to. Heck, he and Paige hadn't grieved their loss together. They held it all inside, unsure how to handle it or how to help the other. He needed someone to talk to. It should be his wife. Paige needed to talk and it should be her husband. Meghan felt stuck in the middle but she was determined to help them. She loved them both and knew how much they meant to each other. Their only problem was communication.

"I'm listening."

"Meg, I don't know what to say to Paige since we lost the baby, and had that terrible argument."

Meghan's heart opened up, sensing his loss and remembering Paige's loss and how hard it was for her. Michael hadn't been there for her; he simply buried himself with the trial. Paige confessed to Meghan through many tears, that he hadn't said a word. She told Meghan she thought it didn't even bother him. They hadn't planned on a baby and the shock hadn't even settled when their loss happened. Paige mourned by herself and then turned to the Spa as an escape from the hurt. He hadn't even consoled his wife when the doctor had told them that there were complications from the miscarriage and they had to perform an emergency hysterectomy. Paige told Meghan it was like he was thankful there wouldn't be any further mistakes. And when Paige brought up the subject of adoption, they'd had that horrible argument. Not a word was discussed again. That's when they began to grow apart and turn to their work. Paige had accepted not having children in the beginning, but with the unexpected pregnancy and then the loss occurred, her biological clock had begun to tick and the idea of a baby surfaced. Alone with that want, that need, it only drove her further into her work.

"Meg? Still there?"

"Michael, you and Paige need to talk."

"I know, I guess I've known that for quite some time. But am I too late Meg?"

"Never too late." Meghan smiled, sensing the love he still held for Paige.

"Thanks, Meg." He sounded more hopeful as though he knew he had a marriage to save and a woman he couldn't live without.

Meghan didn't tell Paige about her phone call to Michael but she was sure he would be back soon to talk to his wife. For now, Meghan wanted to comfort her friend and try to reassure her that she still had a husband who loved and adored her.

It was after two in the morning when Meghan arrived back home and found Eric sleeping. She stood in the bedroom doorway watching him sleep. *God, I love this man. He is so great, I don't want to miss out on this chance I've been given. Why the hell can't I tell him?* Quietly she undressed and gracefully slid into bed next to him. When she wrapped her body around him, he stirred and turned to her.

"How's Paige?"

"Shh..." Meghan placed her finger on his mouth and slowly caressed his bottom lip. One simple touch heightened the desire she felt for him. *Was it lust, love or fate?* At this moment she didn't care. One thing was for sure; she wanted him.

Intense desire definitely could describe what was felt, especially as their bodies moved together. His hands moved from her lower back to her neck. Her hands gently combed through his hair. Not a word was said. Their passion said enough. She kissed his forehead briefly and a tear of joy fell onto his cheek. Her lips slowly followed every curve of his face breathing in the scent of his cologne. Finally her lips met his. No matter how many times had they kissed, every single time was like that first kiss. She opened her eyes to see his eyes filled with tears of delight roving down his face. She kissed each tear and then his eyes softly. She treasured the warmth his love brought her. They made love as if it were the first time they touched. There was content. There was comfort. Maybe one day, Meghan could say the 'L' word.

When Eric awoke the next morning, there was no sign of Meghan besides her scent of raspberries she left in the air, a rose and a note on her pillow.

Good morning, left early for the shop. We have a big wedding party to glamour today. I should be done around two-thirty. I'll miss you, Passionate Kisses, Meg.

Meghan walked into the Spa to see smiles, even Paige's. Her entire staff beamed. *Weddings always bring out the best in people*, Meghan thought as she returned the happiness, smile after smile. Even their welcome sign at the door read 'Today is your Special Day'. Meghan always told her clients whether they were getting married or not, they were to be pampered. Her clients and staff were most important to her. They'd become family. One of her clients had written an article in her magazine about the Spa and how the owners were both professional and personal. The article described Meghan and Paige has two young beautiful happy successful women. It also mentioned they were the envy of most of the women in town. Meghan laughed when Paige read the article to her and said, "It's a good thing they really don't know our secrets. We wouldn't be the envy then."

Meghan snapped out of her thoughts when she heard the wedding party arrive. It was the largest wedding they ever did. Meghan had ordered champagne and fresh fruit for the day. She believed the additional touches enhanced their professionalism. At two-thirty, the bride left in her limo. Meghan's staff looked exhausted. She poured the champagne and toasted to a successful day at Body and Soul Spa before the staff left.

"Paige, how are you holding up? Did you manage to get any sleep?" Meghan asked as she gathered up the champagne flutes.

"No, not really, feeling like I've been thrown aside, like an old pair of shoes." She was comfortable with Meghan and could be herself. Tears fell from her eyes. Meghan set down the champagne flutes and handed her the tissue box.

"I don't know Meg," Paige said as she wiped away the tears, "He seems so different, so distant and he ran so quickly with the Tonia-Opportunity. I don't think he's coming back to me, Meg." The tears flowed and she dropped her head into her hands.

"I don't believe it, Paige. Michael loves you dearly. The sudden rush to Tonia was simply an avoidance to open up his heart, his thoughts. He'll come around once he's thought about it." Meghan tried to console her as best she could.

Paige looked up at Meg, "Maybe Tonia feels the way I do too. She's lost her love. Now I feel guilty for being angry with her. It's not her fault."

Meghan sighed with frustration of the thought that Michael and Paige were so alike. They both still loved one another, yet so damn stubborn to be the first to open up the lines of communication. This thought made her angry with them both.

"Paige, we both know there's no 'lost love' here; it's just both of you being stubborn. Now pull yourself together and get on that phone and tell him that you both need to talk."

Meghan abruptly walked away which left Paige to make the right decision. Meghan knew Paige had to make that phone call to Michael. She knew her friend. It was not in her character to leave unfinished business.

Meghan walked toward her car and stopped in great surprise. Eric stood beside her car with a single red rose in his hand. The sight of him took her breath away. He was the best thing to come into her life in a long time. The feelings of that unknown world raced through her veins. She noticed his eyes locked onto her legs as she walked toward him. The instant they met, so did their lips as they kissed.

"Hungry?" he asked.

"Famished." Meghan smiled and then suggested a quaint romantic bistro by the beach.

They enjoyed a quiet dinner overlooking the ocean. So far their relationship stayed out of the tabloids. Venice was a small town and Meghan had always kept to herself. She'd spent her days with her son. Her only close friend had been Paige. Even at the Spa, she only briefly met their clients. Most of her time was spent in her office or at a seminar out of town, to help enhance their successful business. She usually made dinner for Eric and they ate on her terrace. If they did go out to eat, they avoided the high-peak times.

"Meg, I want to ask you something. You can say 'no' and I will understand." Eric took her hand into his.

She looked at him and smiled. "What is it Eric?" She felt there was something on his mind all through dinner. He seemed a little fidgety at times.

"I've been nominated for the Hollywood Awards," he said humbly.

"That's great news—I think," she said and laughed then confessed she still didn't know much about his world. She never had the time to watch one of his movies. At times she forgot who he really was. "I'll watch your movies one of these days," she promised.

"No worries. I like being your 'ordinary guy.'" He laughed. He filled her in about the awards and that they were known as the pre-Oscar Awards. "You have heard of the Oscars, haven't you?" he asked and chuckled.

She nodded and laughed, "Yes, I'm not completely out of touch with the world".

"I'd be honored if you would come with me," he finally told her.

Meghan didn't answer for a moment. She'd always felt unsure about stepping into his chaotic world. She was a private person. She couldn't even tell him that she loved him and now he wanted her to make a public appearance with him.

"It's okay Meg, if you don't want to. I understand." He gently caressed her hand.

He was always so patient and understanding. She wanted to be with him. She ached when she wasn't. *Maybe it's time to start living my life.* "What would I wear to such an event?" she asked without a second thought. It was time to be brave.

He smiled. "I can take care of that," he assured her.

"What? You're going to pick out a dress for me and I'm to trust you with such a task?" she asked him.

"Yes Meg, I can do that. I have people to help me with such a task," he told her.

"And, if I don't like the dress, I don't go, okay?" She laughed.

"Fair enough." Eric laughed with her.

Chapter Eight

A gentle wind swept through the air, mixing some relief from the sizzling intense heat. Meghan arrived at the Spa early. She hoped Paige had heard from Michael after her sleepless nights of worry. It was usually quiet at this time of the morning with not another soul around. Relaxed and happy, Meghan shifted the car into park, gathered her purse and keys and opened the driver's door. Startled by the man who stood before her, Meghan inhaled quickly and dropped her purse.

"Ben!" "What are you doing here? You're supposed to be in jail." He didn't scare her. In fact, the sight of him appalled her. She didn't feel any affection for him—not since the tragedy; a night she would never forget, never forgive him for. Her support group tried to help her move forward with her life and accept what happened. She still carried the guilt for pushing him to spend time with their son. Meghan couldn't understand how a father, a parent, could not possibly love his own child and not make any effort to spend time with him. She'd been determined to help them form a bond. That night, Ben killed their son.

Meghan remembered the officer saying there was a woman in the other vehicle involved in the accident. Later she discovered the woman to be a single mother of three. Three children almost became orphaned at the hands of her husband.

She'd gone to the hospital that night and found Ben in Intensive Care, hooked up to machines to keep him alive. She wouldn't have recognized him if the nurse hadn't led her to him. His head was covered in a white bandage. Meghan stopped at the doorway and froze. When she looked at him, all she could think of was her son. His life ended at the hands of his own father. His father's stupidity and careless decision to drink and drive killed their only child. The only emotion she felt for her husband at that moment was disgust. Her anger stopped her from entering his room. She'd turned and left. She never spoke to him again.

Meghan didn't go to his sentencing and never visited him in jail. He'd sent her letters that she never opened. To her, he had died along with their son that night. She'd sent their divorce documents on the anniversary of their son's death. There was no love lost; there hadn't been any to hold onto.

Before the tragedy, her husband worked day and night to become a partner at the investment banking firm. He had told her he was building a good life for them. She believed he was selfish and took his wife and child for granted. He had not been a part of their lives. His climb to the top at the bank had only hardened his character. Meghan had no idea he even had the chance of early parole. She had cut off ties with him completely. He was dead to her.

"I was released two days ago. We need to talk, Meg."

"No we don't, Ben."

But he wouldn't take no for an answer. Not now. He pulled the knife from his pocket and forced her back into her car. It shocked her. He was a self-centered man, but this was not in his character. Meghan wondered if prison life had hardened him. Ben climbed into the passenger side and demanded she drive to their cottage.

"Why do you want to go there? You never wanted to go there before," she asked, surprised. She wasn't in fear of her life. She had known him since they were teenagers. This was not like him, but he had rattled her.

"It's the only family home we have left. You sold the other one, but you kept the cottage. That tells me something." He appeared calm but cold. This was not the Ben she once knew and loved.

"I kept the cottage in memory of our son, not you. You never enjoyed it. You only saw it the one time the realtor showed it to us. There's no more family. You took care of that when you made your choice." Meghan kept driving in the direction to the cottage, frustrated. All these years she'd never said anything to him about that night. Now she was ready to release everything she carried inside.

He seemed to pay no attention to her words. It was as if he wasn't listening to her or at least comprehending what she said. "Just drive to our family home."

****

The staff arrived at the spa not long after Ben took Meghan. Lori arrived first to discover the door still locked and the parking lot empty. It was odd. Both owners were usually there. Lori never encountered this before. She called Paige's cell. Paige answered on the fourth ring, "Sorry Lori, I'm on my way". Paige did not want her staff to know about her marital concerns and sleepless nights.

"Thanks Paige. Meghan isn't here either."

Paige asked Lori to call Meghan's cell and gave reassurance she would be there within minutes.

When Lori called Meghan's cell, she could hear a phone ring in the empty quiet parking lot. It was then Lori spotted a purse in Meghan's parking spot. It was Meghan's purse and inside was her cell. Eric's name showed on the display so Lori decided to answer. She hoped Meghan was with him or it was her calling. Eric informed her she had left for the Spa a while ago. Lori told him Meghan's purse was in the parking lot but there was no sign of her or her car. He told her he was on his way and to call the police. Within minutes the police arrived and so did Paige.

Paige decided to close the Spa before clients arrived.

"Lori, contact our clients and reschedule their appointments immediately," Paige asked as the police officers needed to speak to her.

"Can you tell me Meghan Eden's regular routine?" The police officer took notes as Paige spoke.

"Is there anyone you can think of that would want to harm her, or did anyone, including clients, have a problem with her?" Paige informed him that everyone loved Meghan.

"Do you know if Ms. Eden is depressed or if it's possible she's running from a problem?"

Paige almost lost it. He informed her he had to follow through on all possibilities. She calmed and confirmed to him that Meghan's mom had recently passed. "Meghan was grieving as anyone would but not to the point she was suicidal."

"Is she married, single, involved and does she have any children?" The police officer drilled one question after another.

"Divorced, involved. She had one child who died years ago," Paige informed him quickly. She wanted Meghan found.

"Who is Ms. Eden involved with?"

"Eric Nolan." The police officer stopped writing and looked at Paige.

"The movie star?"

"Yes."

The officer excused himself and informed her he had to talk to the detective in charge, who had just arrived. Paige watched as the detective and the officer spoke. Her cell phone rang and made her jump.

"Eric, I'm worried something has happened to Meg. I was late this morning. I should have been here when she arrived."

"Don't blame yourself Paige. Maybe she forgot something. This may turn out to be something as simple as that. Are the police there? What have they said?"

"Yes they are here. They haven't said anything. They've just asked a lot of questions. Are you almost here?" She looked up to find the detective standing before her. "Eric, I have to go. Hurry."

"Mrs. Adams, I'm Detective Johnson. May I ask you a few more questions?"

"Yes. Of course Detective Johnson, do you know something new?" Paige motioned for him to join her on the sofa. He appeared professional and compassionate to Paige.

"Ms. Eden's ex-husband is Ben Eden, is that correct?"

"Yes."

"He was sentenced to a prison term for manslaughter for the death of their son. Is that correct?"

"Yes, but what does this have to do with anything?" Paige knew it was known in their community but it had been so long ago. Meghan moved on with her life, divorcing Ben years ago. She had never spoken to him since that night. Actually, Meghan didn't want his name mentioned at all. Paige respected her best friend's wishes and never spoke of him.

"Did you know, or more so, did Ms. Eden know Ben was released on early parole two days ago?"

Paige's jaw dropped and she stood up, "What?"

"I'll take that as a no, you did not know."

Paige ran her hand through her hair trying to absorb what she just heard. They never spoke of him. It had been so long she had become accustomed to believing Ben no longer existed. This news was a surprise. Detective Johnson walked away from Paige and called in an APB on Ben Eden and asked to be put in contact with his parole officer. When the detective walked away, Paige called Eric back.

"Any news?" Eric asked without even saying hello.

"Their point of interest is Ben Eden. He was released from prison two days ago," Paige informed Eric.

"Meg never said anything. Do you think she's with him?"

"Not by choice. We never spoke about him. She told me she never wanted to hear his name again. She received letters but always tossed them out. I respected her wishes."

"Do you think he would have taken her? Oh my God Paige! Do you think he'd hurt her?" Eric's tone seemed anxious and worried.

"Oh God Eric, I hope not! He wasn't that kind of man before, but I don't know what prison has done to him. Are you almost here?"

"I'll be coming through the door in a minute."

Paige felt some relief. She couldn't get in touch with Michael but had left him a message. She didn't want to go through this alone. She let her staff go home when the police finished questioning them. They had contacted their clients and rescheduled. It was hard trying to hold it all together and think of the business at a time like this, but she was a strong woman.

The detective told Paige he'd received a call from Ben's parole officer who met with Ben yesterday and was due to check in with him soon. If he heard from Ben he promised to contact the detective right away. Detective Johnson informed Paige he was going to Ben's place to check it out and gave her his card if Meghan showed up or she thought of anything else that could help. "Mrs. Adams, would Ms. Eden voluntarily go with Mr. Eden?"

"No!"

"Is there any place you can think of that he would take her to? Is there any place of importance to them?"

"Meg sold their family home after her son's death. They both grew up back east. Would he take her there?"

"Not likely. He's got no means to go too far."

"Maybe the grave site of their son," Paige thought out loud. The detective made a note but as he started to walk away, Paige said, "Wait a minute, detective. They own a cottage on the beach but it was of no importance to Ben, only Meg and her son."

"This information could help Mrs. Adams. Where is it located?"

Eric walked into the shop as Paige gave the detective the address of the cottage. He went to Paige and they hugged, then he asked her for her car keys. She handed them to him without hesitation and he walked out. Paige called out his name but he didn't answer. The detective turned when she called out Eric's name. Detective Johnson motioned to one of the officers and told him to follow Eric Nolan. Then he called in a possible kidnapping.

"Detective…" Paige was worried and confused.

"Thank you for your help, Mrs. Adams. I will let you know as soon as I have any more information for you. Will you be here?"

Paige nodded. She wasn't going anywhere until she heard of Meghan's safety. Her cell phone rang after the detective left.

"Oh, thank god Michael!" She'd left him a frantic message to call, saying it was urgent.

"Paige, what's wrong?"

"Meg is missing. Her car is missing. Her purse was left in the parking lot. And Ben was let out on early parole two days ago. The detective was just here and headed to Meg's cottage. They think he may have taken her there. Can you come home?" She wondered if he heard the fear and worry in her voice. She was a strong woman, but she needed him.

"On my way, Paige."

He wasn't going to let her down. "Thank you Michael, I need you."

"I love you, Paige."

Paige smiled for the first time since she got the call this morning. He did love her. She hadn't lost her husband after all. They just had a rough spot to get through. "I love you Michael," she answered.

Angela Ford

Chapter Nine

Meghan shifted the car into Park and turned off the ignition. "Well, we're here. What could you possibly want to talk about it Ben?"

"We'll talk inside." There was no emotion in his words, his expression still cold. Meghan still felt more frustration than fear. She got out of the car and walked ahead of him. She unlocked the cottage door and walked in, leaving it open. She just wanted to get this conversation over with and hopefully never see him again. She had put him out of her mind completely and kept no memory of him.

"So? What do you want to talk about?" "And for Christ's sake Ben, put the damn knife away!"

He continued not to show any emotion when he set the knife on the counter. "Meg, I want your forgiveness and to get back what I had."

"That will never happen. What you had? Exactly! What you had was being selfish and distant," she reminded him. She sat down and threw her arms into the air as she said it. She was irritated but calm. There was a moment of silence and Meg turned and looked at him. "You killed our son," she added.

Angela Ford

"It was an accident," he said in a voice that showed no signs of guilt. Ben never really got to know his son. His selfish climb to the top kept him from that. Meghan thought prison must have hardened him and her rejection of him fueled his anger.

"It was your choice to drink, your choice to drive with our son in the car. Ben, what were you thinking?" she demanded.

"I thought I was fine."

His simple reply only confirmed his selfishness to her. *He hasn't changed.* She rose from the chair. Now she was angry and mere inches away from him. "You thought you were fine! You had our son in the car! You weren't socializing with clients! You were supposed to be bonding with your son—you know, that little person who didn't know who you were because partners and clients always came first? Ben, does *any* part of you feel remorse?"

He remained quiet with a cold, somber expression.

"They charged you with manslaughter and attempted manslaughter of that poor woman you almost killed and made three children orphans. Remember her Ben?" Meghan no longer felt calm. And she knew he could hear it in her raised voice.

"You abandoned me, Meg. I've lost everything because of you. I married you when you got pregnant. I

92

took you with me to the west coast. I provided for you and gave you everything I could. It was never enough. You never appreciated it. You never supported me working so hard to get that partnership. You pushed. Why couldn't you just be happy for me and take care of the kid?" he finally replied.

His words infuriated her. *Selfish bastard! He can't even acknowledge his own son's name and that he took his life!* Before she could say a word, he grabbed her arms and pulled her in close to him. His lips pressed hard against hers. Pulling back, she slapped him across the face. "Don't ever touch me again!"

She tried to walk away from him and he pulled her back, tightening his grip on her arm. "Let go Ben, you're hurting me!"

"And you haven't hurt me?" he shouted angrily.

Ben reached back for the knife. Meghan watched his action and she raised her knee to his groin to startle him and kick the knife out of his hand. She started to run toward the front door when she heard the gun shot. Ben lost his balance with her kick and grabbed his backpack as he fell. He had opened it and pulled out the gun. She froze, not knowing whether she'd been hit. The echo of the shot was so loud, it deafened her and she couldn't hear. Her breaths grew quicker. Her heart pounded faster.

"You're not going anywhere Meg until you apologize."

She turned her head slowly. He stood pointing a gun in her direction.

"Come back here." His tone was cold and demanding. This was not the man she had married. She wondered who he'd become.

Meghan turned. Now she felt fear. "Ben, don't do this. This is not you."

"You did this to me Meg. You left me. I lost everything because of you. Now apologize."

She tried to convince herself he would not hurt her. "Ben, think about this. This isn't going to make me apologize or forgive you."

"Then it's over, for both of us."

Oh God! What does he mean? He wants to kill us both?

****

Eric ignored the police car behind him, the sirens and lights. Detective Johnson wasn't far behind. Eric saw Meghan's car and pulled in behind it. He ran up the steps of the porch and froze when he heard Meghan scream "No!" Then he heard the sound of a gunshot. The police officers had caught up with him and forced him aside. They drew their guns and announced their presence. There was silence. One officer kicked in the door while the other officer motioned for Eric to stand back. He didn't stand back. He raced in after the second officer entered and saw her knelt down over Ben's body and shaking uncontrollably.

"Meg."

She turned when she heard his voice. She didn't speak. He helped her up and held her tightly then walked her out to the porch to get her away from it all. Detective Johnson arrived as they walked out onto the porch. Eric took her off to the side away from the door. The detective gave Eric a nod and entered the cottage. Detective Johnson spoke with his officers. They reported they arrived too late, heard a woman call out and then heard the gunshot as they reached the door. He had them call it in and went back outside to Eric and Meghan.

"Ms. Eden, I'm Detective Johnson. I'm glad you're not hurt. I know this is difficult, but I need to ask you a few questions."

"Can't this wait?" Eric barked at him.

Meghan withdrew from Eric's hold. "It's okay Eric." Still shaking, she held tightly to Eric's hand and walked over to a porch chair. Detective Johnson took a seat beside her while Eric knelt down in front of Meghan holding onto her hand. He placed his other hand on top of hers and caressed it gently.

"You had us worried. I'm glad you're safe. I am sorry this had to happen to you but I have to ask you a few questions while the events are still fresh in your mind. We will need you to come down to the precinct to give a statement," Detective Johnson said in a compassionate voice. Meghan nodded in agreement.

"Meg! I was so worried!" Meghan ran into Paige's arms at the police precinct.

"Paige, he wanted me to apologize for ruining his life. I refused. I thought he was going to kill us both." Meghan broke down in her friend's arms.

"Maybe if I had talked to him instead of walking away, he would have understood." Meghan desperately fought to understand why he took his own life.

"I don't think so, honey. Don't let him throw you back into a guilt trip." Paige told her.

"She's right, Ms. Eden. There's nothing you could have said or done to change his mind. He may have fooled the parole board into believing he was a changed man, but his actions proved otherwise." Detective Johnson spoke sincerely and Meghan turned to him and smiled. "I know this is difficult but I have to ask you to give your statement now."

Meghan turned to Eric. He wrapped his arms around her in a comforting embrace and kissed her head. She looked up at him and smiled to tell him she was thankful he was there. She followed Detective Johnson down the hall.

Eric turned to Paige, "I don't know what to say to her Paige".

"Just be there for her Eric. She needs you. Ben didn't want back what he had; he simply wanted to punish her for her decision to leave him. He had been selfish to the last act." Paige locked her arm in Eric's and led him to the waiting area while Meghan gave her statement.

****

Meghan walked onto her terrace and sat quietly. Eric asked her if she wanted something to eat. She shook her head. Eric poured her a drink and handed it to her. That she accepted.

"I was so worried today Meg, that something happened to you. Then when I heard that gunshot, my worst fear set in." The compassion in his voice touched her heart. She looked up at him. His eyes - watered.

She was still trying to piece the day together. It seemed like a dream; even more so a nightmare. He gently touched her arm. She felt comfort and decided it was time to share her past with him. Her eyes focused straight ahead at the sunset and began to tell him the story of her past.

"Ben was my high school sweetheart. I got pregnant our senior year and we married after graduation. He received a scholarship for his athletic ability. I was more focused on little Ben, whereas Ben was more focused on playing sports and studying. Ben suffered an injury that ended his sports career but his degree in business landed him a position with an investment bank in Venice, California and that's why we moved here."

"Ben always worked. He said he was working toward a partnership offer. He had always been competitive and determined. I supported him and tried to accept the fact that he wasn't around for us, and mostly for his own son. He was growing up without knowing his father."

She stopped talking for a moment. Eric reached out for her hand and stroked it gently. Meghan smiled. A tear fell upon her cheek and he brushed it away, but he remained quiet and just listened.

"It was hard Eric, to see my son's hurt every time he fought for his father's attention. That night I pushed and begged Ben to take his son to the ball game. It was a bad decision. That night took my son. I've carried the guilt for so long. If only I hadn't forced Ben to take him, my son might be..." Meghan couldn't get any more words out. Tears slid down the side of her face. Eric took her hands and stood. He held her tight while she cried.

"I wish I could have been there to comfort you then. I'm glad you had Paige," he told her.

Meghan's cries calmed. "We hadn't known each other for long but she was my tower of strength. I don't know how I would have survived it without her," she told Eric.

"Missing him?" Eric asked.

"Always," she replied in a soft voice.

He continued to hold her in his arms. The strong yet gentle embrace made Meghan feel glad she'd finally shared the story with him. *I hope I never stop missing him.*

He whispered in her ear as if he had read her mind. "Keep him in your heart. Your memories will never fade. I'm always here to listen whenever you want to talk about him." He placed his hands on her face and kissed her.

"How did I ever get so lucky to find you?"

"No," he replied, "I'm the lucky one." He gently wiped away the tears that fell on her face. Meghan's heart skipped a beat. She knew deep within her soul how much he cared for her. His eyes began to water.

"Oh, please, don't you start crying." Meghan barely touched his eyes.

"I can only imagine the pain you carry in your heart."

He was so tender and caring. How could she possibly withhold anything from him any longer? She knew it was time to open her heart to him. She felt safe and trusted him completely. She had shared her past, her pain. Now it was time to share her life, her love.

"Eric?"

"Yes, sweet?" he replied. He took her hands into his.

She smiled at his reply, "I like it when you call me, 'sweet.'" He raised her hands to meet his mouth and kissed her fingers, one at a time.

"Do you remember when we first met at the golf resort in Arizona?"

"I remember you standing there looking at me and not saying a word."

He laughed and nodded in agreement with her. "Yes, but when you turned to me, you caught me off-guard with those big beautiful blue eyes. It was probably the first time anyone ever made me speechless. Those eyes drew me to a place I'd never dreamed of before: so beautiful, so peaceful. I loved you at that moment. I know how that sounds, but you made me feel things I have never felt before. You captured my heart right then and there. He placed his hand over his heart. I knew I'd forever be at your beck and call." He laughed.

Meghan laughed along with him. "I had that effect on you?"

"Yes, ma'am."

"Is that why you call me sweet?" Meghan was still a little confused about how 'sweet' fit in.

"No, actually, it was when we stopped for lunch and we ordered coffee." Meghan just looked at him. "I offered cream and sugar for your coffee and you replied, just cream, I'm sweet enough."

Meghan remembered and smiled. She thought of her mom. "It's an old saying I got from my mom." She knew for certain she was ready. She withdrew from his embrace and looked deeply in his eyes.
"I love you Eric"

She saw the tears in his eyes when he smiled and said, "I love you Meg."

Meghan finally opened her heart to Eric, completely and it now belonged to him. "Would you like to see a photo book of little Ben?" she asked.

"I would like that." Eric smiled then followed her down the hall.

She asked him to sit down on the bed. She walked to her closet and reached for a box. "This is little Ben's baby album. I made it like a storybook so that when he was blessed with his own child he would have this to share." Tears began to fall upon her cheeks. She knew that would never happen. But Eric encouraged her to continue with the simple gesture of wiping away her tears. He placed his arm around her and she opened the album. Tears fell as she flipped from page to page, but she smiled at the memories. A proud and loving mother, she thoroughly described each picture. When Meghan closed the album, she let out a sigh. One of remembrance, but also one of relief as she realized her memories would never fade.

Eric gently kissed her face. "Thank you."

Meghan turned to him. "For what?"

"For sharing something so special with me, he was a lucky boy to have you for a mom."

She touched the side of his face with one finger. "You are the special one. Eric, you are so patient with me."

"Don't ever let go Meghan. Keep the good memories in your heart forever," he said and placed his hand over her heart.

"And let go of the guilt," she added.

"You're not the one to blame Meg. You were only trying to make your son happy and help him bond with his father. It was Ben's choice to drink and drive. It was his choice to take his own life. You can't blame yourself." Eric reached for her hand.

"I know. I just wish I hadn't made him take Ben to the game. I should have known that he didn't want to. I knew I couldn't make him love his own son or want to spend time with him. I just hated seeing my son so hurt." Meghan dropped her head onto Eric's shoulder while the tears streamed down her face.

"It's not your fault, Meg. You loved your son," Eric said, and she knew he tried to comfort her.

She reached for him and pulled him into an embrace. The hint of his cologne gave her comfort as he held her. She could feel his heart beat against hers. Her feelings for him were so strong, they soared through her. He held her in his arms and she cried herself to sleep.

Chapter Ten

Paige paced at the arrivals area of the airport, anticipating Michael's walk through those doors. It had only been a couple of days, but they had been distant a long time. She loved him with her whole heart. She needed him. For the first time she admitted that to herself, and to him. It was time they grieved the loss of their baby, together.

The door opened. It was Michael. She ran to him and threw her arms around him. He gently kissed her. "Paige, I've missed us."

Paige was about to speak when she noticed that a man stood beside Michael.

"Paige, this is my old dear friend from London, Bill Lyndon," Michael introduced him. Paige shook his hand. She wondered if they had run into each other on the flight.

"Shall we get a drink?" Bill asked them and motioned to the lounge. They ordered their drinks and Michael took Paige's hand in his,

"Paige, Bill is not only an old friend but is a lawyer who concentrates on adoptions."

Paige felt confused, "Michael, I thought you didn't want to discuss adoption after our loss." She remembered the pain of losing their baby and the devastation to discover that complications prevented her from another pregnancy.

"I know," he said as he continued to hold her hand. "I wanted to give you time to grieve. We should have grieved together and I'm sorry for that." With tears in his eyes he went on, "I felt you thought that I was relieved because I hadn't been too enthused about the pregnancy. I probably wasn't. The thought of having our baby suddenly struck my heart and then it was too late. I was devastated but I wanted to be strong for you. I was wrong. I wasn't there for you at all. I want to make it up to you now. I love you so much."

Paige wiped away his tears and hers. "Michael, I love you. The past is in the past."

He reached for both her hands. "Paige, will you have a baby with me?" he asked.

"I would love to have a baby with you Michael, but—"

She was interrupted by Bill Lyndon. "There are legal papers to sign and then you will have your baby girl in two weeks," he announced.

Paige looked at Michael and Bill. "Wait a minute. How is it possible for this to happen in two weeks? Doesn't it usually take a long time?"

Michael confessed, "I ran into Bill shortly after our loss and he gave me the idea. I wanted to tell you when it was for certain. I didn't want you to suffer any more disappointment."

Paige kissed her husband tenderly. "You did this for me." Her eyes filled with tears of happiness.

"For you *and* for us," he replied. "You're not mad I did this, are you?" he asked.

"No Michael, thank you," she said softly and turned to Bill. "Now where are those papers we have to sign?" Paige wiped away her tears.

Michael and Paige signed all legal documents and thanked Bill. Then Paige embraced her husband. He kissed her forehead and placed his hands tenderly on her face. He then kissed her passionately and she quickly realized their love had not been lost.

"Let's go home." Paige smiled.

****

Eric turned when Meghan entered the kitchen. "Hey sweet. You look rested."

"Something smells good." She smiled.

"I'm making breakfast for you."

She walked toward his open arms. The warmth of his embrace comforted her. His scent relaxed her.

"Just you being here helps." A smile crossed his face. Eric was all she needed. "I've decided to go back to work tomorrow and get on with my life." This time she was not going to carry guilt around with her. There was nothing she could have done to stop Ben. Even the apology he asked for. She smiled content with herself, her life. She knew Eric had to leave soon. The Awards night was approaching and he had to return to take care of a few things. "I'm still coming for the Awards night. Do you have the dress you promised me?"

Eric smiled. "It's good to hear you talk this way." He held her tight. "I do have a dress hanging in my closet with your name on it." He smiled. "I love you Meg."

"I love you too, Eric." She nuzzled between his head and shoulder, breathing in his scent deeper, feeling the warmth from his protective embrace. She wanted him. His body could never lie to her. She felt his hard body against her when she shifted closer to him. "Make love to me," she whispered in his ear. She took his hand and he followed her to the bedroom. She no longer shied away from him. He had been so patient. He stood by her through rough times and he loved her. She was blessed with this second chance, with Eric.

Meghan turned at the doorway and focused on the motion of his lips parting. They exchanged seductive smiles. She longed for those lips. She could no longer resist. His hands moved to her waist and she swayed with the brush of her hips against him. She took it to the next step and deepened the kiss. Her hips pressed tighter against him and she heard soft moans of pleasure through their kiss. She felt his faded blue jeans stretching their limit. The excitement she was building appeared unbearable. Her ice blue sundress shoved above her thighs as she moved over him. The thin straps of her dress on her shoulders fell to leave a glimpse of her breasts that rose and fell with every breath. She began to unbutton his shirt slowly, one button at a time. She could tell by the hunger in his eyes that she was about to drive him over the edge. He tugged at his shirt to free it from his jeans. She surprised him with her assertiveness when she stopped his tugging and ripped his shirt open. Letting the remaining buttons fly across the room. Aggressively she pulled his shirt over his broad shoulders. He heard a soft seductive wish to remove her dress and it fell to the floor. She leaned in closer and pressed against his bare chest. Their hearts beat strong against each other. She wanted to excite him the way he always excited her. She ravished the side of his neck with deep passionate kisses and traced his neckline with her tongue to his ear. She whispered, "I want to please you."

"You are definitely pleasing me Meg."

She loved the way he said her name, especially when he was lost in their world. Meghan directed him to the bed. She commanded him to take off her panties.

She felt his fingers stumble as he tried to grab them. She heard him grumble something about removing his jeans. "I don't know how much more I can take Meg."

"No more clothes off yet until I take care of this edge," she said with a devilish look in her eyes. He agreed not to argue with this woman.

Her lips parted longing for his kiss and he accepted the invitation. She tasted him as she nibbled softly along his bottom lip, taunting and teasing him. He grabbed her hand and moved it along his chest, over his tight abs to where she met the denim of his jeans and its restricting tightness. She sat hugging his hips with her thighs.

"Meg," he uttered nearly inaudible. It appeared he was losing control. Her plan was working. She had him exactly where she wanted him and whispered against a kiss.

"Just let go," she commanded him. She tightened her grasp. Her moist flesh burned through his jeans. He bit his lip and his hands squeezed her thighs. Her body shook as she cried out his name. He held onto her firmly as he let go. A few moments of silence followed when Meghan broke the silence. "Yes?'"

"Meg," he barely whispered as though trying to catch his breath, "'No other woman has ever done that for me".

She smiled with great satisfaction.

"I've never ever experienced pleasure like that." He kissed her tenderly.

She threw him one of those sweet smiles and then surprised him with her next comment.

"It did take the edge away, but I'm not done with you yet." They had not moved. There were moments of silence before she confidently began to seduce him all over again. He sighed with pleasure and watched her hand slide passionately back down to the stiffened denim. "Meg you are amazing."

She glanced up for only a second and smiled. She slid off his lap and knelt before him. He moaned with her actions. Her hands unfastened the button of his jeans and as she unzipped them. He threw his head back, closing his eyes and bit his lip as she took him slowly and erotically back into their world. He barely heard her next command but obliged.

"Lift up," she ordered.

His hands pressed behind him against the bed as he lifted his hips. She undressed him and admired his muscular hard body. Her hands pushed his thighs further apart. She nestled in between. His hands gently grabbed her hair. As promised, she began to take him to another release. When her lips touched the tip, he called out her name. He shifted his body to move with her. Her tongue slid up and down so slowly he quivered.

She devoured him. One hand gripped along with her mouth, her other hand on the inside of his thigh. She could feel his heat. Unbelievable desire roared as he let out a cry of pleasure. He tried to push her away but it was too late. Her tight grip on him led him into a wild uncontrollable explosion.

She gave him a moment to enjoy the experience before she raised her head and looked into his eyes. She watched him carefully as he slowly opened his eyes and discovered she was back on his lap gazing into his eyes with a smile of satisfaction. She allowed him time to come back to reality before she threw him her next remark. "Successful so far?"

"Oh yeah." She got up and stood before him. He looked up at her, "I take it you are not done with me yet?"

She smiled. The view of her quickly removed any thought he had of not being able to continue.

"Ready?"

He looked at her.

"Have you forgotten already?"

"U-uh ..." he stuttered. It appeared she caused a blockage in his capability to speak. She reminded him that he had promised to make love to her.

"Oh, I'm definitely not going anywhere." He kissed the tip of her finger that moved slowly across his bottom lip. "And I never back out of a promise."

Chapter Eleven

Meghan pulled into her parking spot and just sat quietly for a few moments. Thoughts of Ben raced through her mind. She slowly turned to take in her surroundings. Paige's car was all she noticed. *Snap out of it Meg, and get on with your life.*

"My, aren't we happy this morning?" Meghan walked through the front doors to find Paige watering the plants and humming along.

"Meg, how are you feeling?" She set down the water canister.

"Better. I've decided I'm not going to sit around and feel sorry for myself or waste time searching why Ben did this. I'm going to live my life. I've decided to go to the Awards. I want to be there for Eric," Meghan replied.

"I'm proud of you Meg. I hoped you wouldn't blame yourself again." Paige hugged her.

"So what has put you in such a great mood? I'm hoping Michael is back." Meghan withdrew from their hug.

"He is." Paige grinned.

"Everything is good?" Meghan hoped so.

"Oh, Meg, it's better than good. I have so much to tell you."

Meghan looked at her watch. They had time before their staff arrived. "Coffee on?" she asked.

Meghan found Paige in her office, still smiling. She set their coffee mugs on the desk, "Do tell." Meghan smiled. Paige shared her exciting news about the baby. The news filled Meghan's heart. She was delighted for her best friend.

"I knew it would work out, babe. Michael adores you. Sometimes it is just hard to open up, even to those you love." Meghan knew firsthand what that meant.

"I take that smile on your face is not only for my happiness. Am I wrong to assume you finally took your own advice?" Paige raised her eyebrow with that certain tone Meghan knew all too well.

"Paige, you better remain seated for this one. I said it."

"Said what?"

"I told him I love him."

Paige smiled. "I knew you would."

"I'm so thrilled you decided to go to the awards Meg. What are you going to wear?"

"So am I. Don't worry Paige, I won't forget the little people in my life." She laughed as she held her hand over her heart. Then confessed, "Well, I agreed to let Eric get my dress."

"Wait a minute. You seriously will let Eric pick out your dress?" Paige raised that eyebrow again. "Honey, the thought of a man, no matter how much you love him, in charge of such a task could be disastrous." Paige shook her head. Meghan laughed. Her best friend could be so dramatic at times.

"He offered, and then I dared him with the option if I didn't like the dress I didn't have to go." But Meghan felt a little worried as well. "What have I agreed to? But then again he did state he knew a designer to help him. I trust him with the task. I'm actually looking forward to the surprise."

The sound of the phone and the buzz of staff as they entered the shop quickly ended their time alone.

"I'll grab the phone Meg," Paige announced. Meghan headed toward their staff who practically tackled her down with hugs. Within minutes they were back to business.

Thoughts of Eric raced through Meghan's mind all day while she worked. His lips, his touch... it was difficult at times to remain focused. She missed him already and hoped the next couple of days went by fast. Paige was no different. Every time Meghan passed her office, she noticed her smiling.

Meghan took time that morning to call her dad before he heard the news about Ben.

"Are you okay Meggie?" Her dad was shocked at the news.

"I'm fine Dad. I've finally realized I can't blame myself anymore for Ben's decisions or actions. I've decided to move on with my life and not let that second chance get away."

"I'm happy to hear you say that. Your mom would be pleased. She wanted you to be happy, as do I."

Meghan told him about going to the Hollywood Awards with Eric. He promised to watch and was going to tell all his friends to watch for his Meggie on the red carpet. She promised to keep in touch and tell him all about it.

Meghan decided a hot bath would relax her when she got home. Completely relaxed, continued thoughts of Eric still raced through her mind. What had he done to her strength, her control? Heck! She no longer even considered trying to overcome it. She had never before in her life even dreamed of a man touching her the way he did. Eric had taught her, shown her, what passion could be. Her mind drifted back to when she had initiated their lovemaking. She brought him pleasure, selflessly touching him in ways that turned his fantasies into reality. She not only loved him, but she hungered for him. Her body ached for his touch. Her thoughts left as the water cooled. She reached for her robe. She had planned to watch the sun set. The phone rang.

"Hey, Sweet," Meghan smiled at the sound of that deep husky voice. God! Even his voice made her ready for him.

"Eric, I was just thinking about you." She chuckled silently.

"I hope it was naughty."

"Actually, yes." She spoke in complete confidence. She shocked herself.

"Oh? What are you wearing?"

Meghan laughed like a child, ready to play with him. "Well, I hate to disappoint you, but I'm wearing my white fluffy robe."

He didn't laugh; he simply continued the conversation in a restrained voice. "And underneath?" he devilishly asked.

"Well now, that may excite you." She paused, and then answered him, "Nothing at all."

She heard him sigh, and then he said, "I miss you Meg. I wish I was there to explore what's underneath that robe."

Meghan smiled. His comment made her ache even more for him now. "Eric, I miss you. I've ached for you all day," she confessed.

"Shall I take off the edge?"

"I wish you could." She knew he remembered her exact words. Her body trembled. She missed him so much she wished he would change the subject before she crawled out of her skin.

"Where are you?" he asked.

"Enjoying the view with my wine." She felt relieved he changed the subject. The view was amazing that night. The full moon shone upon the darkened ocean. The waves rippled where the cruise ship passed. But it remained still and peaceful as if it had not been touched. She almost choked on her sip of wine with his next comment.

"Remove the robe."

"What! And stand here naked before the world?" The shyness in her hadn't completely disappeared yet he continued to play with her.

"I'm imagining that robe piled around your feet at the floor. I'm serious Meg. You have more than enough of a private view. No one can see you. Except for me when I close my eyes."

"Eric!" She laughed light-heartedly.

"Let me take the edge away Meg," he pleaded with her. "Consider it payback time. I want to return the favor Meg. And I did promise I'd find a private place for *this* chat." Meghan remembered when she told him

Paige thought they were having phone sex. She didn't know if he was serious or just playing with her.

"Over the phone, Eric? Yeah, right."

"Never had phone sex?" He laughed.

Meghan wondered how far he was willing to take the game. She did admit to herself it was beginning to fire up curiosity and excitement. *He can't be serious.* She quickly answered him with an innocent, "No, Never".

"Let me be the first," he whispered an unselfish offering to her. "I want to be the first to give you a gift no other has."

"Can't be done," she argued. The possibility of it seemed rather unattainable, yet on the other hand, her ache for him was unbearable.

"Oh yes it can." He sounded determined.

There was a brief pause, and he could hear her breathing. She was considering it. "I can tell by your breathing that you're considering it." "Come on Meg, be a good sport. Give me a shot at it." He gave it a last try. Another pause, a quick sigh and she agreed.

"Okay, I'm game. Give it your best shot. I still think you are crazy. This won't work." She was curious to see if he was serious or just playing. He was serious and determined. A pause came over the phone and she only heard his breathing. Then she heard him ask her to remove the robe and let it drop to the floor.

Oh god, the man is serious. She wondered if she could go through with this. She had no choice; she'd agreed to this crazy plan and she never backed out of a promise. Without a word spoken she heard him ask her to put down the phone and switch it to speakerphone. Then he told her to place her hands on the window above her head. She followed his lead, not saying a word. She had promised to let him give it his best shot. The sound of his deep sexy voice alone increased her breathing, enhanced her aching body to want this. Her shyness and her innocence had disappeared. She trusted this man and her curiosity heightened with anticipation as to whether he could succeed.

A soft moan came from deep in his throat as he spoke to her seductively. She closed her eyes. It was like he was actually there with her. She could feel his presence. He definitely could read her mind. He asked her to close her eyes and imagine him in the room standing behind her from this moment on. She envisioned his reflection in the window and him whispering in the dark. He told her he was only inches away from her and could see her pinned against the window naked. Her body trembled, aching for him. She imagined his hardened naked body close to her. She barely heard him whisper he was moving slowly towards her. It was unbelievable how reality had disappeared. His words, his presence had strengthened.

He told her his body barely touched hers but he could feel the heat from her. She heard him continue, as though he was really there.

"My hands slowly embrace your waist. I feel your soft, silky skin through my fingers. Oh! Meg, you feel amazing to me. My fingers travel around to your belly. I feel you shiver with anticipation as my fingers reach up to your hardened tips. Yes, I feel your excitement. I can feel how much you want my touch. I'm cupping your breasts, playing with them, teasing you with sudden short touches at the tips and then leaving them. Leaving you in anguish of your wanting, needing me to touch them again. My hands travel south to your thighs. I feel your hips sway as I pass them. I feel the heat, the moisture near your thighs. Your breathing is heavy. You silently demand me to move my fingers to your hot flesh. You are so hot Meg, so wet. You are driving me crazy. I can feel you move with my every touch, demanding my finger to slightly cross over your hot flesh again. Your body shivers as I follow your demand. My finger travels down and slips in. Meg you are so hot, so wet. Another finger joins in and you welcome that with the shift of your body, pushing hard against me. The palm of my hand rubs against you. You push harder, faster. Your body is trembling. Your belly is aching, burning. How much more can I take before I explode is racing through your thoughts. The rhythm is building the anticipation of satisfaction. You are working harder for that, you push harder and faster. Your breathing has turned into gasps of air as your mind has forgotten to breathe. The only thing on your mind is that orgasm you are working for. You are incredibly wet. Your heat is burning me. You just can't seem to get enough as you ..."

He stopped talking and smiled. He gave her a few moments to come back to reality. Then he asked, "Yes?""

"Wow!" she responded.

"I'll take that as a yes. And Meg?"

"Yes," she could barely utter.

"I win," he said and laughed.

She came back to reality. Her shyness reminded her of what had just happened. She knew her view was a private one but she still looked around, hoping no once had seen her.

"You definitely win," she laughed in embarrassment.

"Well, I think we both win this time Meg."

"Yes, I can agree with you on that one." She sighed with great relief.

"A definite orgasmic experience?" he asked.

She smiled. "Oh yes! I never imagined a phone call could be so pleasurable." Her body and mind were in awe.

"Sweet dreams, my sweet," he whispered.

"What about you?" she asked.

"I'm taking matters into my own hands," he said with a chuckle.

Chapter Twelve

"I'm surprised. You haven't forgotten the little people in your life," Paige teased Meghan when she answered her phone.

Meghan laughed at her comment. "I could never forget you, Paige."

"So, how were the Awards? Who did you meet? What were they like?" Paige asked with enthusiasm.

"It was an incredible night, Paige."

"You looked incredible, Meg. I take back that it wasn't a good idea to have a man pick out the dress. Eric did well."

"He definitely did."

"When I saw you walk the red carpet on Eric's arm, I stood up cheering so loud, Michael thought I was going to have a heart attack." Paige laughed.

Meghan could picture her dramatic friend and laughed. "Should I let him pick out the wedding dress too?" she asked.

"What?"

"He proposed."

"Oh my God. He proposed!" Paige yelled out. "I'm so happy for you, for you both."

"Will you be me by maid of honor?" Meghan asked.

"Yes, of course. Will you be my little girl's godmother?"

"Yes Paige, I'm so excited for us both."

"Me too. See you in two days."

Meghan hung up the phone and looked up. There he was standing in the doorway, with a single red rose between his teeth. She smiled. She had only left him long enough to give Paige a quick call.

He walked toward her and gently placed his finger on her lips, caressing them. He slowly leaned down to meet them with his. "I missed you," he said.

"I missed you too," she replied and their lips met again.

"Now that I've gotten my kiss, I'm going to jump in the shower before dinner. You can join me if you like." Eric threw her a bashful smile.

"Now there's an offer I can't refuse," Meghan said and followed.

Meghan put on Eric's white pajama top after their long shower, and met him in the kitchen. He was wearing the bottoms. His tanned muscular body drove her crazy. "Dinner in half hour sweet," he said as he leaned over to kiss her. He handed her a glass of wine and held his up, "To us." He gently pulled her close until their lips met. They had dinner on the patio to enjoy a beautiful sunset. After dinner he took her hand and she followed him to the bedroom.

Meghan and Eric flew back the next day and spent the afternoon baby shopping. Meghan was throwing Paige a surprise baby shower the next morning at the shop. Because she was exhausted from shopping and decorating the spa that night, Eric offered to get take-out for them. Meghan had some quiet time and decided to call her dad with her latest news. She had promised to keep in touch with him.

"Meggie, what a pleasant surprise," he said when he answered the phone.

"I have some exciting news to share with you," Meghan said.

"I did see you walk the red carpet," her dad said.

"Oh, that." She tried to laugh it off, in modesty. "I want to tell you about that night too dad, but first I have to tell you that Eric——."

"Eric proposed."

"Yes. How did you know?" she asked.

"A handsome gentleman showed up at my door last week and asked permission for your hand in marriage. I was touched that still happened. He couldn't stay long. He had business in New York to attend to but we had a wonderful chat. I like him, Meggie. Your mom would have loved him."

"I like him too, Dad." Meghan smiled and they chatted for awhile about the awards night.

Paige arrived at the shop Tuesday morning to discover a surprise baby shower. She thanked Meghan. "I can't believe you did this, and there's everything here I'll need."

"Well, you know me Paige, born to shop. I hope you like everything I picked out... well with Eric's help. I think he actually had more fun than me," Meg remarked.

"Will you help me set up the nursery?" Paige asked her.

"I'm there," Meghan promised.

They worked day and night on the nursery. Most women had nine months to prepare, but Paige had one week. Eric told Meghan he couldn't resist being close to his beautiful fiancée and stayed to help. Meghan told Paige one night in the nursery that she believed Eric's biological clock was ticking. Paige laughed as she looked over to see Eric and Michael playing with the baby toys. "And yours isn't," Paige asked her.

Meghan rolled her eyes at Paige. "I'm just getting used to the idea of having one other person in my life besides me!" They laughed.

Eric moved over to the laughter, put his arms around Meghan and kissed her on the head, "What's so funny over here ladies?" Paige told him she was wondering if all this baby stuff was getting Meghan's biological clock ticking. "What's so funny about that? I think it's getting mine ticking," he said.

The women burst into laughter at that remark.

"You two are definitely made for each other." Paige shook her head and walked over to Michael and kissed him.

Meghan turned to kiss Eric and he said, "So?"

"So what?" she asked. "A baby. Do you think we'll have a baby someday?" Eric looked into her eyes.

"Someday. We have a wedding to plan first," Meghan reminded him. He kissed her again.

Eric opened a bottle of wine when they got back to the condo. "Let's start planning," he announced to Meghan.

"On a baby?" Meghan asked. "Ah! You are thinking baby, but I meant the wedding. Although, I can promise we can start practicing on making a baby." Eric smiled at her with a bashful look. They decided on a beach wedding at the beach house. It was large enough to entertain a couple of hundred guests. The guest list was finalized and Eric asked if he could surprise Meghan with the remaining plans. He promised her a most beautiful magical wedding.

"What, no dress this time?" She laughed.

"No, that's your department. I can't see the dress before you walk down the aisle." She promised to wear a gown that would knock him off his feet.

"All I want right now is to see you wearing nothing at all," he said and whisked her off to bed and got his wish. She seductively removed his clothing piece by piece. Then she proceeded to undress right before his very eyes, slowly to drive him crazy with each article of clothing she removed. She met him on the bed. His mouth opened as he moved in closer, their bodies touched. Her tongue reached the depths of his mouth. He whispered her name through the kiss. She told him what she wanted and was definitely going to get it. Her control made him desire her more. He reached for her and pulled her in closer. "You drive me crazy," he whispered in the dark.

"Make love to me Eric," she demanded.

He made love to her like he'd never loved another woman. She fell asleep in his arms. He lay there for a while and watched her. He kissed her forehead and softly whispered, "Good night sweet. I promise to always love you."

The phone rang early the next morning. It was an enthusiastic Paige. It was 'baby' day.

"Just making sure you and Eric are still coming over," Paige said.

"We wouldn't miss it for the world, but baby doesn't arrive until noon," Meghan said.

"Yes, but I want you both here sooner... like now!" Paige said. Meghan could feel the excitement in her voice. She looked at Eric." She wants us over right away."

Eric smiled, "Let's go then."

They arrived at Paige's an hour later to a wonderful surprise wedding shower. Paige had prepared a champagne breakfast for Meghan and Eric and their friends.

"Paige, you shouldn't have done this, but I love you for it." Meghan hugged her friend.

"I wanted to do this for you and Eric. After noon today, I'll be a little busy."

Every guest brought a piece of lingerie for the honeymoon. Paige walked over to Eric and put her arm around him. "Guess you'll be fairly busy on that honeymoon," she said and they both laughed.

The doorbell rang.

"Baby." Paige ran for the front door. She opened the door and there she was, Paige's little princess, so beautiful. Paige's eyes filled with tears as she held her baby for the first time. Michael leaned over and kissed their new baby girl on the head ever so gently. The two proud parents entered the room where all their friends waited. Michael announced, "Everyone, Paige and I are pleased to introduce you to Meghan Brooke. We've decided to name her after the person who has been such an important part of our lives—her godmother Meghan."

Michael gently placed baby Meggie in Meghan's arms and kissed her on the cheek. Meghan cried, "I don't know what to say. I'm so honored. Thank you both."

Eric walked over to Meghan, kissing her first and then little Meggie. "Okay, let me have a turn now," Eric said like an impatient child at Christmas.

Meghan smiled and gently handed him the baby. She looked at him. She fell in love with him all over again by the way he held the baby. *He would make a wonderful daddy, s*he thought as she watched him.

"How about a walk on the beach?" Meghan asked Eric when they got back to the condo.

"I'd love to do anything with you," he replied moving closer to her, rubbing his nose softly against hers and then kissing her. They walked hand and hand and barefoot along the beach. Meghan remarked how comfortable he seemed when he held the baby.

"I never imagined how wonderful it would feel to hold someone so small, so beautiful and innocent," Eric replied with a grin. Meghan noticed the sparkle in his eyes.

"Meg, I never thought about it before. I never thought I would ever say this. My focus has been on my career. I want a baby." Eric stopped, held both her hands, and looked into her eyes. She smiled.

"I think you'll be a wonderful father someday. Can I ask you a favor?"

"Anything," he replied.

"Eric, you've made me so happy, you've given me so much. I never went to my senior prom because I was a new mom and wife. The Awards the other night, and that dress made up for that loss. My wedding to Ben in my mom's living room only consisted of my parents and his. It was a marriage that should never have happened. I want to do it right this time. I'm asking you for our wedding first, and then with all my heart I want to have our baby."

Eric kissed her and told her he understood. He promised to give her the wedding of her dreams. Eric put his arms playfully around her waist and moved in closer to meet her lips. He stood back and looked into her eyes without a word. He appeared lost in thought.

"What's on your mind?" she asked.

He smiled. "We only have a couple of hours before my flight," he replied and then she knew what was on his mind.

She took him by the hand and led him back to the condo. There was only one place she wanted to be before he left. He said he wanted to make love to her slowly so the memory would linger in his thoughts all week. His lips passionately encircled hers. She sighed with delight. She shifted desperately trying to touch him but he kept his body just inches from her. He was definitely taking it slow and driving her crazy. He took the kiss further. His hands placed on either side of her head and held his weight to keep his body barely touching hers. The kiss was intense. He stopped briefly and looked into her eyes. The passion in his eyes made her want him more. His lips parted and without a word, met hers again. His weight shifted when one hand traveled to lift her sundress. He barely touched her skin with the tips of his fingers. Her breathing was heavy. Her heart was pounding. Her hips moved desperately to get any touch of him. She watched his eyes travel over her body. "Make love to me now, Eric." He removed what remaining clothing was left. Passion grew and tension subsided. Meghan's body moved in sync with his and they became one body, one soul.

On the way to the airport, they talked about the wedding plans they'd started and realized they hadn't set a date.

"How about New Year's Eve with fireworks on the beach?" he suggested.

"Sounds fabulous." Meghan smiled and leaned over to kiss him. "And, now you are on your own with the planning," she reminded him.

"You must really trust me." He smiled and kissed her again.

"With my life." She waved goodbye as he walked through the departure gate. Her heart ached when she couldn't see him any longer. The airport partings were getting harder each time.

Paige waited at her condo door when she got home. "Is everything okay?" she asked. Meghan wondered why she was there now without the baby.

Paige reassured her with a smile. "Life couldn't be better. I have to talk to you about something and I wanted to do it in person," Paige answered.

Intrigued, Meghan said, "Come in then. Glass of wine?" Meghan asked.

"Yeah, thanks," Paige replied fidgeting.

Meghan took Paige's hand. "What is it honey? You know you can tell me anything."

Paige took a deep breath. "Meg, you are my dearest friend. I love you so much. You are the best partner I could ever dream possible. Now that Meggie has come in to my life, I can't imagine being apart from her. I want to be there for her, I don't want someone else raising her—"

Meghan interrupted, "Say no more, I know how you feel. I've been there. I'm so happy you've made this decision. You'll never regret it. You deserve to be with your little treasure. Promise me you'll enjoy every single moment with her."

Paige hugged her, "Thanks babe. I thought I might hurt your feelings leaving the business."

"You'll never hurt me. We may no longer be business partners, but we'll always be friends and in each other's lives." Meghan hugged her friend.

"Are you sure you're okay with this?" Paige asked.

"Yes. Actually, I'm a little relieved," Meghan replied.

"Relieved?" Paige looked at her.

"Yes, I've wanted to talk to you too. But with the baby on the way, I was afraid I'd hurt your feelings," Meghan confessed.

"You want out too?" Paige asked her.
Meghan then told her she wanted to be with Eric and they would like to have a baby too.

"I'm so happy for you Meg. You deserve this!" Paige exclaimed. "Meg, I was nervous to come and talk to you, but I'm glad I did," she admitted.

"I'm glad you did too. Now get back to my god-daughter. She needs you," Meghan told her and smiled.

The next morning Meghan announced to the staff at the Spa that Paige decided not to return to work and stay home with Meggie. Her next comment to them was tough and she took a deep breath before she told them they were going to sell the Spa. She listened while they responded with mixed emotions. They appeared to be devastated to lose Meghan and Paige but happy for both of them.

Eric called the Spa at lunch time, but Meghan was at the realtors. She returned his call when she got back. "Sorry I missed your call earlier," she said when he answered.

"They said you were at the realtors." Meghan had told him about Paige's visit but he sounded surprised they were going to sell the business so quickly.

"I didn't want to wait. I can't stand saying goodbye at the airport any longer. I know we haven't discussed where we would live after the wedding, but I'd like to live at the beach home," she told him.

"Meg, I'm so happy to hear you say that. I love you. I love the idea of you wanting to be here with me. Are you sure that you want to give up your business?" he asked.

"I've never been more certain of anything in my life. I want you, and hopefully our baby someday," she told him.

"You have made me a very happy man. I promise to make you a very happy woman. I love you Meg."

"I love you Eric. You already do."

Chapter Thirteen

Eric knew the first thing he had to do was hire a wedding planner. The one person he trusted to help him find one was his agent.

"So, what did you think about the script?" Adam asked without a 'hello.' Adam Baker was one of the top agents in L.A. for many famous actors. He signed million dollar deals over a martini. He was the best. That's why Eric fought for him when he first started in the business. If there was one person who knew anybody in Hollywood and their connections, it was Adam Baker.

"Haven't read it yet, but I need your help." Eric had the script for the past couple of weeks. He knew Adam expected him to have read it by now and ready to give his opinion. Adam told him it was a great opportunity and he could get him big bucks on this one. Eric felt tired. He had done two movies in just over a year. The last one had given him one award and Adam was certain it would lead to an Oscar for Best Actor. Eric had succeeded as an actor and his success was hard-earned. He was wanted in the movie industry and producers were willing to pay whatever it cost to get him.

"You haven't read it yet? I should have never tracked down that woman for you," Adam said sarcastically. It sounded more like a reprimand to Eric, and he was about to get shit for not following Adam's orders.

"'That woman has a name. It's Meghan, and she's my fiancée," Eric corrected him, rather harshly.

"Sorry man. Good choice, by the way. She looked great on your arm on the red carpet."

"Is that all you think about? The next deal and appearances?" Eric barked at him.

"Yes." Adam was honest about his business. That's why million dollar deals were signed if you had him as your agent.

"You can be a cold bastard at times, you know." Eric laughed. There were times he knew he would not get one ounce of human compassion from this man.

Adam laughed. "Yeah, that's why you have me. Now what about this script? I need an answer."

"Can't do it now, I'm getting married," Eric answered.

"So? People get married every day. And, divorced the next. What's your point, Eric?"

Eric wondered why he trusted this man. There never seemed to be any human nature in him whatsoever.

"I can't start a movie in December. I'm getting married New Year's Eve," Eric informed him.

"I can get them to wait until January," Adam replied coldly.

"You are priceless." Eric chuckled.

"There's usually at least six figures on the check," Adam's inflated ego spoke for him.

There was no way Eric would get married and leave Meg the next day to start a movie, so he began to bargain with Adam. "Get them to start in February and I'll read it for you this week."

"You're pushing it now man, but I'll give it my best shot. You'll get the bill for these drinks." Adam laughed.

"I always do." Adam charged every last little expense to his clients.

"So what can I help you with?" Not only was Adam good at getting deals, he wore many hats when it came to his clients. He would do anything for them as long as he took their advice when it came to getting the deal signed.

"I need a wedding planner."

"A wedding planner? Why doesn't she take care of that?" Adam asked.

"I promised a magical wedding. She deserves it. I want to do this and you're going to help me," Eric replied.

"I'll get you the best, but that's the extent of my part in this wedding." Adam paused. "Though this could bring good exposure for you," Adam remarked, business always at the forefront of his brain.

"No exposure. I mean it," Eric told him.

"Think you're a little late for that, my friend," Adam stated.

"Meaning what?" Eric asked.

"Am I the only one who reads the tabloids?" Adam already knew that answer. He always told his clients not to read them. He tried his best to keep his clients out of the line of fire but it was Hollywood and they were in the limelight. Adam told Eric that Meghan's 'little escapade', had hit the stands. Adam informed him everybody wanted to know who the woman on Eric Nolan's arm was.

"Fortunately for them they were able to get the latest scoop from her small town. The tabloids show a picture of Meghan on your arm on the red carpet. Husband holds her at gun-point just days before...Now she's in Eric Nolan's arms...Who is she?'" Adam read to Eric what one tabloid had written. He told Eric they were all basically the same with the same picture. "We need good exposure now Eric," Adam reminded him.

"Shit!" Eric ended the call without saying good-bye. He immediately called Meg.

"Hey Eric, I was just about to call you. We got an offer on the Spa."

Before Meghan could continue, Eric interrupted and told her the bad news. "I'm sorry, sweet. It leaked after the Awards. Guess they wanted to know who you were."

"Oh God, Eric, how did they get that information?"

"They always find a way, Meg. I'm so sorry. I've tried to keep you away from this crazy chaotic world I live in. It will die down quickly. I'm refusing any movie from now on," he promised.

"Eric, this isn't your fault. You and Paige both told me not to carry the blame for what happened. I'm not. Neither should you. You can't just give up your dream. Not for me. I won't let you," she pleaded.

"You are too important to me Meg. I don't want this for you or for our child someday. I've decided to send Adam on a new quest. I want to produce, that's what I always wanted," Eric told her.

Meghan wasn't about to argue with him. Not now. They both needed time to digest the leak and hope it quickly became old news. She reassured him her support and love with whatever decision he made. She asked what she should do for the time being. Eric said he was going to tighten security and send a bodyguard her way. She thought he was being a little over-protective but she let him make the decisions. She had never been in a situation like this before. Eric said he was grateful she was with Michael and Paige when he asked where she was. Eric asked to speak to Michael. Then Meghan filled Paige in.

Michael passed the phone back to Meghan. She walked to the other side of the office to speak quietly with Eric. She felt somewhat reassured after the call ended. Eric would be coming the next day and a bodyguard would be at Michael and Paige's within a few hours. Michael agreed with Eric that Meghan should stay with them. He promised Eric to protect Meghan against the paparazzi. Michael ended the call with Eric and made another quick call while the women chatted.

"Meghan, you will come home with us tonight. Eric will be here in the morning. Both of us want you to be safe until this blows over," Michael announced after his call.

"It's not necessary, Michael. I'll be fine. I'll just stay in tonight," Meghan told him.

"Meg, I just got off the phone with your condo security. The paparazzi are already camped at the door waiting for you," Michael informed her.

"What? Oh my God." Meghan had to sit down again. Michael then informed them that Eric had a bodyguard on his way and he'd just spoken with Detective Johnson about sending a patrol car to the house—just to be safe.

"Do you think they'll come to our house?" Paige asked frantically. "We have to get home to Meggie," Paige said and grabbed her purse.

"I can't go with you two. I'm not putting Meggie in any type of jeopardy," Meghan said.

Michael told them both they were leaving the office with him and everything would be fine. Meghan felt relieved they closed the Spa early that day to meet with the prospective buyers. She felt hesitant as they got in Michael's car, but Paige assured her she would feel better if she knew they were all together at home with Meggie.

When they arrived at Paige and Michael's house, they were met by Detective Johnson. He had come for the first shift himself. He told them he hoped someone in his precinct hadn't leaked the information. Detective Johnson had the case sealed by a judge to protect the parties involved. It was a small town and it didn't take long for gossip to travel. Meghan and Eric's relationship had been kept quiet up till then.

"Do you think it may have been one of the staff?" Paige asked Meghan, after picking Meggie up in her arms.

"Does it even matter at this point? Eric said it would become boring to the paparazzi and die down. I hope he's right Paige. I hate putting you through all this."

Paige smiled at her. "Don't worry honey, it will go away soon." She went to give Meggie her bath. Michael was still outside chatting with Detective Johnson. No paparazzi had shown at the house and Detective Johnson told Michael the police car should keep them away. Meghan went to put some coffee on. It appeared she wasn't going to get much sleep that night.

Michael found her in the kitchen, "Where's Paige?" he asked.

"Giving that sweet baby girl her bath." Meghan smiled and handed Michael a coffee. Meggie definitely had a way of taking anyone's stress away. Michael excused himself and told Meghan he was going to see his girls. She loved hearing him call them 'his girls.' "Michael?"

He turned around before leaving the kitchen. "You okay Meg?" he asked.

"I'll be fine. I just wanted to say I was sorry for putting you through this," she apologized.

"Don't even think twice about it Meg, you're family. I wouldn't have it any other way." He smiled. Meghan was thankful she had them in her life. The doorbell rang as Michael left the kitchen. He told

Meghan he would get the door and for her or Paige not to answer the door or the phone. She smiled and thanked him.

Detective Johnson was at the door with a man. He introduced him as Paul Dawson, the bodyguard Eric had sent. The detective assured Michael he checked his identification and credentials before bringing him to the front door. Michael shook Paul's hand and invited him in. He reminded Detective Johnson not to hesitate if he needed anything, and thanked him. Michael directed Paul to the kitchen and introduced him to Meghan.

Eric arrived early the next morning and Meghan ran into his arms. "I'm sorry Meg."

She told him not to worry, that they would get through this. "Nothing can come between us Eric. Look at everything we've already survived. You have been patient with me. I will be patient. I know this will go away soon." She kissed him. She didn't care who was in the room.

Meggie was the one to break the silence and the kiss with her baby sounds. They all laughed. Meghan's phone rang and Michael picked it up. Still in protective mode, he looked at the display. "Meg, it's your dad."

"Shit, I forgot to call him last night. I hope he hasn't seen the tabloids." Meghan pressed the button to answer his call. She walked into the other room to privately tell her dad what had happened. She was right.

He had seen the tabloids and was concerned for his daughter. She reassured him that Eric and Michael had taken care of her protection from the paparazzi. He told her to thank them for him. Meghan knew her dad could handle any reporters at his end. She told him she would call in a day or so and that hopefully by then, it would quiet down.

Angela Ford

Chapter Fourteen

Within a week the paparazzi had given up as Eric said they would. The incident with Ben had been the only worthwhile tidbit of gossip on the couple and the media moved on to more dramatic couples. Meghan was thankful. The wedding was only two months away but she felt safe enough not to postpone it. Eric believed there wouldn't even be interest in their wedding, "We're now known as a dull couple".

"I like it that way," Meghan laughed.

Eric had turned down the movie. He told his Adam he would keep him as his agent if he could help him get into production. The offer for the Spa was accepted and signed within a month, despite the incident with the paparazzi. Michael told Paige and Meghan that the incident actually intrigued the buyers. The two couples celebrated to new beginnings. Meghan had successfully sold her condo and had stayed back to complete both closings. She promised Eric she would have everything completed and moved into the beach house by the end of the month.

A month had passed but it felt like a lifetime. Eric was waiting at the airport for her with a single red rose.

When he seen her walk through the arrivals-door, he knew how lucky he was to have her in his life. He embraced her with a passionate kiss.

Eric paused from the kiss for a moment. "I can't believe you're finally here."

"Forever," she replied and kissed him again.

A trail of rose petals led to the bedroom and had been tossed all over the bed. Eric had a bottle of champagne on ice beside the bed and on the bed were their favorite white pajamas. He had their names stitched on them. She turned to Eric and he smiled. He moved in closer and placed his hands on her face and kissed her passionately. Together they undressed each other between kisses.

Meghan awoke and found Eric watching her. She smiled. "Morning. I know now there is nothing in the world I could possibly want or need but your love."

"Morning sweet. You definitely have it." He kissed her on the forehead. "Hungry?" he asked.

"Starving."

After her shower she met him, wearing the white pajama top, on the terrace. He was having a coffee, and reading the newspaper. She walked up behind him and wrapped her arms around him. She kissed him on top of his head. "I love you," she said.

"I love you too, sweet." He reached up for her hand and brought it to his lips. Meghan poured a coffee and grabbed a bagel. Eric put down the paper. "I thought we'd go shopping today," he said.

"I love to shop. What we are shopping for?" Meghan asked as she ate her bagel.

"We have an appointment with the wedding planner first. I'd like you to meet her, see what she does, and then I promise the rest will be a surprise. I want to take you shopping for whatever you need or want to make you comfortable here. It's your place too."

Meghan smiled. "I'd love to meet the wedding planner, but I don't think there's anything I need. I already feel comfortable here with you."

"Well then, I guess we'll just shop for whatever pleases you. He grinned.

"You are spoiling me." Meghan walked over to him and sat on his lap.

"Get used to it." He smiled and kissed her.

They drove up the coast and stopped at a beach home. There were parked cars everywhere. Meghan commented that this wedding planner must be really busy.

Eric opened the car door for her and took her hand. "Actually, this is a wedding."

Meghan felt confused. "Are we dressed for this?" She looked at them both dressed in blue jeans and T-shirts.

Eric smiled as they walked toward the house. "We're just here to meet the wedding planner. This is how she sells her services. If you like what she does, you hire her".

Meghan thought, *Things are certainly done different in this part of the world,* but just smiled at Eric.

The wedding planner was buzzing around when Eric pointed her out to Meghan. She wondered how the woman moved so fast in those heels. Even in heels, she barely reached over five feet tall. She had amazing great legs. Leila was a beautiful woman, dressed to perfection in her lilac designer suit and matching Gucci shoes. She wore her jet-black hair with beautiful red-violet shades of highlights neatly piled in a twist on top of her head. Meghan was shocked when Leila opened her blazer to a strapped compartment on her waist. Meghan wasn't sure exactly what she had there but it seemed to hold a lot. The flower girl stood before Leila with a scraped knee and tears in her eyes. Leila quickly grabbed a tissue for the sweet little girl and a band aid after spraying the little girl's knee with what Meghan assumed was an antiseptic spray. She seemed so calm and sent the happy little girl on her way. Leila closed her blazer and adjusted her headset without anyone appearing to notice. Suddenly, Leila began to speak into her headset and noticed Meghan and Eric standing close to her. She smiled at them and continued to speak. It appeared she was telling the father of the bride what to say as he toasted his daughter.

Meghan spoke up when she finished. "Did you just tell him what to say?"

Leila smiled and reached her hand out to Meghan.

"You must be Meghan. Eric was right. Your eyes are more beautiful than the ocean. And yes, I helped him with his speech. He was a little nervous and wanted to make this a very special day for his daughter." She then shook hands with Eric. "Nice to see you again Eric. Come, I'll show you around."

Eric and Meghan followed her. She asked what Meghan felt was most important about their wedding. Eric thanked her for her time and reminded her that it was still a surprise for Meghan and it had to be perfect. She reassured him it would be.

"So, what do you think of Leila?" Eric asked as he opened the car door for Meghan.

"A little eccentric but adorable." Meghan wasn't quite sure what to think of her. They had only spent a few minutes with her, but Meghan thought she was amazing. When she had asked Meghan what she wanted for her wedding, Meghan simply told her she wanted a fairy tale magical wedding on the beach. From those few words, Leila quickly came up with a description that captured Meghan's mind and took her away into a dream. "I have no worries that she will make my dream a perfect reality." Meghan smiled.

"My first thought of Leila was the same, Meg," Eric confessed. He laughed and told her about his first meeting with Leila and how she had requested him to meet her at one of her weddings. "I knew by the end of our meeting she was the one to make our perfect magical wedding."

"You weren't joking when you said you loved to shop," Eric laughed as he tried to unlock the door with many bags in-hand. "I never joke about shopping," Meghan smiled.

"I'm exhausted, I need a shower." Eric set the bags on their bed. Yet, when Meghan joined him in the shower; he appeared to have gained his second-wind.

Eric met with the wedding planner every day without Meghan to keep it a surprise. He had left the honeymoon plans up to Meghan, and of course, the perfect dress. This time the dress was a surprise for him. All he knew about the honeymoon was that it was at the golf resort in Arizona where they had met. He was concerned when he overheard Meghan on the phone one evening in tears. "The wedding is a month away and I still haven't found my perfect dress."

"Thanks Paige, you're the best." Meghan ended her call

"Everything okay Meg?" Eric kissed the top of her head. She looked up at him with tear-filled eyes, "Just a little trouble finding a dress".

"I can help." He took her by the hand and into his arms. "I'll call Leila."

"I didn't think it would be so hard to find a dress so I called Paige," she confessed as she released from his embrace.

"Is she coming?" Eric asked.

"Yes, tomorrow."

"Good. I let Leila know. I'm sure they will both be a great help. Feel better?" He kissed her and she smiled and nodded.

He put a call into Leila, their savior. Leila called Meghan the next day and gave her an address for a wedding boutique where they could meet. Meghan picked Paige up at the airport and they went directly to the boutique.

****

Meghan looked at Paige's expression when they entered the boutique and saw Leila move so fast while she rambled to the sales lady. The women watched in awe as the sales lady frantically retrieved the dresses Leila pointed out.

"Is that your wedding planner?" Paige pointed toward Leila.

"The one and only, Leila. I know she's a little eccentric but she's the best," Meghan remembered her first impression of Leila and laughed.

"A little?" Paige laughed.

"Oh Meghan darling, come here." Leila waved the ladies over and kissed Meghan on each cheek and then took notice of Paige. "And this must be the best friend Paige?" Leila gave Paige a barely-there hug and kissed each cheek as well. Then she was off again in a ramble about the dresses. She spoke so fast, no one else got a word in.

"This is the fairy tale bridal collection. Perfect for your wedding, Meghan," Leila announced.

"I like this one," Leila had the sales lady hold up the dress. "It's a mermaid-style gown of draped satin and lace, with an organza rosette pick-up skirt and a chapel train." Meghan knew it was her perfect dress the moment Leila said, "That dress will definitely make the difference when the officiator announces, 'you may now kiss the bride'".

"You are amazing." Meghan threw her arms around Leila. The words 'that kiss' had never left Meghan's mind— that kiss in Arizona and the many more passionate ones that followed. Meghan found the perfect dress.

"Perfect choice Meghan. It reminds me of your joie de vivre." Leila smiled.

Paige asked what she said. Leila translated that it meant 'joy of living.' "Wow, you are amazing. That definitely describes Meghan."

"Let's go to lunch and celebrate." Leila said in excitement after all measurements had been taken.

Chapter Fifteen

Meghan picked her dad up at the airport the night before the wedding.

"Aren't you coming in Meggie?" her dad asked when Eric met them outside the beach house.

"I've been given strict orders not to enter the house until tomorrow," she laughed.

"What? No rehearsal?" he looked puzzled.

"I've been given strict orders not to reveal any detail of this surprise magical wedding to your daughter. All you have to do is follow my orders and walk her down the aisle to Eric."

He nodded in agreement. "That I can do".

Meghan introduced her dad to Leila and told him she was their wedding planner. The look on her dad's face made her laugh. Everyone had the same expression when they first met Leila. Eric grabbed the suitcase from the trunk and offered Meghan's dad a drink. He then kissed Meghan good-bye and assured her he would take care of her dad.

The day - finally arrived. Leila - succeeded in an extravagant private wedding - perfect for both Eric and Meghan. Michael joined Eric for a drink on the terrace. "I've never seen such a calm groom."

"I'm marrying the perfect woman," Eric replied and smiled confidently.

Leila waited at the front door for the limo to arrive. "Meghan, welcome to your magical wedding." Meghan's eyes lit up and filled with tears. "It feels like I'm walking into a dream, a fairy-tale." Meghan walked through rose petals scattered about the entrance.

"I'm honored to hear you say that," Leila placed her hand over her heart. She then directed them upstairs to get dressed. She promised to meet them upstairs as soon as she checked on the final touches and greeted the guests.

Paige had tears in her eyes when Meghan appeared in her gown. "You are the most beautiful bride. You are definitely going to knock him off his feet!" she said and they both laughed.

"Unforgettable." Leila stood at the door and smiled. "We are ready to begin," she announced. Meghan met her dad at the top of the staircase. He smiled.

"Meggie, you are so beautiful. You deserve this happiness. Hold it close to your heart, always."

Meghan smiled. She definitely was going to take his advice and hold it very close to her heart.

She got to the terrace door and gasped, "This is amazing". She couldn't believe her eyes. A tunnel of little white lights sparkled like the stars. There was a red carpet that led the way to the beach.

This is it. It's time, Meghan thought as she walked down the red carpet. She walked with confidence. She was happy and in love with the man waiting at the end of the carpet for her, and locked her eyes on him. He stood waiting for her, holding a single red rose. His hand reached out to hers. She placed hers in his. Forever.

ABOUT THE AUTHOR

Angela Ford originates from Nova Scotia…Canada's Ocean Playground! Her love of the ocean and sunsets are always in her heart and give her inspiration. Her love for words keeps her turning the page. She is never without a book, whether she's reading or writing. Now residing in Ontario, Angela works in Finance – numbers by day – words by night. Her dedication to volunteer and involvement with cyber safety seminars gave her an Award of Distinction and sparked the idea for her first book *Closure* – suspense with a dash of romance that hit the best- selling Action/Adventure. Her newest release, *Unforgettable Kiss*, delivers a romance with a dash of suspense. Between two jobs, being a mom with a home always filled with teenagers and rather interesting stories; she is lucky to have one very patient and understanding man. But it is the fury family members who rule the house – a Puggle, two loveable cats and two unique Guinea Pigs. Every possible quiet moment she finds, she treasures and just writes about the moments to come. Angela is an avid reader of romance, a member of the RWA and thrilled to be part of her new family BTGN. You can follow her at BTGN www.bookstogonow.com or www.angelaford.net to connect with her on her social network sites. She loves to hear from her readers – they keep her smiling!

29716112R00095

Made in the USA
Charleston, SC
20 May 2014